WALKING ACROSS EGYPT

Clyde Edgerton

WALKING ACROSS EGYPT

A Novel

Algonquin Books of Chapel Hill   1987

Published by
Algonquin Books of Chapel Hill
Post Office Box 2225
Chapel Hill, North Carolina 27515–2225

in association with
Taylor Publishing Company
1550 West Mockingbird Lane
Dallas, Texas 75235

Design by Molly Renda.

Library of Congress Cataloging-in-Publication Data

Edgerton, Clyde, 1944—
  Walking across Egypt.
  I. Title.
PS3555.D47W3 1987   813'.54   86-20645
ISBN 0-912697-51-2

In memory of Lex Mathews

I

The dog was a tan fice—cowlicked, thin pointed sticks for legs, a pointed little face with powerful whiskers, one ear flopped and one straight.

He was lying on the back steps of Mattie Rigsbee's brick ranch one summer Saturday morning when she opened the door to throw out a pan of table scraps for the birds. She placed her foot on the step beside him. She was wearing the leather shoes she'd cut slits in for her corns. The dog didn't move. Holding the bowl, Mattie stepped on out into the yard and tried to see if it was a him or her so she could decide whether or not it *would* have been possible to keep it if she were younger and more able. If it insisted on staying she'd have to call the dogcatcher because she was too old to look after a dog—

with everything else she had to do to keep up the house and yard. She was, after all, seventy-eight, lived alone, and was—as she kept having to explain—slowing down. Yet her neighbor, Alora Swanson, was fond of saying, "Yeah, she cuts her own grass, and keeps that place looking better than I would, or *could*." Alora liked to tell about how Mattie fell in the kitchen and fractured her hip when she was seventy-six and then worked around the house for two weeks before finally, after a sleepless night, consenting to go to the doctor—who had to put a pin in. And during those two weeks Mattie picked butterbeans at least four or five times. After the pin was in, Alora would say: "Mattie, I told you it was broke. I told her it was broke," she would say, looking around. "I said, 'Mattie, it could be broke. You better go to the doctor.' But she wouldn't go. You know Mattie."

The dog, lying on the steps with Mattie bending over trying to see if it was a male, looked sick. It had no spunk—wouldn't even get up so she could see if it was a male or not.

"Well, bless your little heart," said Mattie. "Where in the world did you come from?" The tip of the dog's tail moved once. "Are you hungry, Punkie? You look kind of skinny." The dog snapped at a fly. "I guess I'll have to fix you up a little something to eat."

The dog sat up slowly.

"Well, I'll declare," said Mattie, "you *are* a male."

Back inside, Mattie put the bird bowl in its place by the sink, bent over and pulled out the cast-iron frying pan which she declared was getting too heavy for her.

She then warmed some beef stew and water, poured it into a small bowl over two opened biscuits cooked that morning, and started outside with it. Maybe he's gone, she thought. She wanted him to be gone so she wouldn't have to put up with him until she called the dogcatcher. She would have run him off if he hadn't been so skinny and lacking in spunk.

The dog had not left. Mattie put the bowl down a few feet away so he would have to walk and she could tell if he'd been hit by a car. He stood, walked over to the bowl and with large gulps ate all the food. He looked up at Mattie when he finished.

"You ain't been hit," said Mattie.

When Robert, Mattie's forty-three-year-old unmarried son who ran the Convenient Food Mart in Bethel, fifteen miles away, came that afternoon—he usually dropped by on Saturdays—he said, "Mama, what in the world do you think? Of course he ain't going nowhere after you *feed* him." Robert and Mattie were in the kitchen.

"Well, he was so skinny."

"He's skinny because he's got worms. Look at his eyes." Robert, thirty pounds overweight and graying at his temples, ate from a bowl holding a big piece of apple pie and three scoops of vanilla ice cream.

"I know how to tell worms," said Mattie.

"He's got worms." His mother was going to stand right there and not believe the dog had worms when anybody could look at the dog's eyes and tell he had worms. Why couldn't she just relax and say, "Okay, he's got worms"?

She was standing at the counter, dipping a scoop of ice cream for herself, wearing the brown button-up sweater, unbuttoned, with the hole in the elbow, that she'd been wearing every day, summer or winter, until at least mid-morning for . . . Robert knew for ten years at least. "I don't know if he has or not," she said.

"Okay, Mama." Robert had recently read an article in *Parade* magazine which explained how grown children could avoid misunderstandings with their parents. It said to give up trying to change them. So he decided to give up on the worm argument even though he knew he was right.

"I couldn't just chase him off," said Mattie, "as skinny as he is."

Robert, holding pie and ice cream in his spoon over the bowl, looked at her. "But now you're going to call the dogcatcher?"

"You know I can't keep a dog."

"Why not?" Robert wished she could get a little company, companionship of some sort. Something to care for. An animal maybe, a parakeet. He spooned the pie and ice cream into his mouth.

Mattie turned to look at her son. "With all I got to do around this place? Besides, I'm slowing down."

"All you'd have to do is feed him," said Robert, pie crust on his lower lip.

"Use your napkin. You know it takes more than feeding to keep a dog. I got as much business keeping a dog as I got walking across Egypt. I don't even know why I'm talking about it."

Monday morning, Mattie called Bill Yeats and asked him to come get her chair bottoms. She wanted the bottoms of her four kitchen-table chairs and her den-rocker bottom re-covered with some kind of oil cloth. They were looking so dingy and she needed something she could just wipe off without worrying about it.

Bill said he'd come after lunch. Mattie told him to come around eleven-thirty and she'd have a little bite for him to eat. There was that chicken in the refrigerator. He said he'd be there.

She decided she needed a couple of short boards—so she could place them across the open bottoms of the two chairs she used most often—her kitchen chair and the den rocker. If she put it off she might forget and fall through a chair. She had some boards in the garage. She walked out the back door. She limped slightly from the hip fracture, but, as usual, walked with purpose, her brown sweater hiked up in the rear.

The dog was in the back of the garage. Mattie had refused to name him because of her plans to call the dogcatcher. He got up and walked toward her. Looked like he had gained a little weight over the last day or two, but still he didn't have much spunk. He'd been eating regular for two days now and he did not have worms. Robert jumped to conclusions.

Mattie found two short boards in the back of the garage, started back to the house, stopped and said to the dog, "Listen, I'm going to have to call the dogcatcher. I don't have time for a dog. Shouldn't have kept you this long."

She brought the two boards into the house, then decided she might as well go ahead and take the chair bottoms out and put the boards across two kitchen chairs. Bill would be there before long. She could have everything ready when he came. They would have a little more time to sit and talk. It was just four screws per chair. Bill would be impressed. She'd put on the chicken and then do it. After it cooked, she could give the neck meat to the dog—with some gravy and a biscuit or two. She ought'n to spoil him though, she thought.

She spooned grease into the frying pan, cut up and washed the chicken, salted and peppered it, rolled it in flour, and placed it in the frying pan, piece by piece. Then she got her screwdriver, carried each of the kitchen-table chairs past the kitchen counter over to the couch in the den, dragged over the rocker from in front of the TV, sat down on the couch, turned each of the kitchen chairs upside down, unscrewed the screws, and took the bottoms out. The rocker was a little more difficult. It was heavy for one thing. She turned it onto its side and unscrewed the screws, which were larger than the others, and tighter.

When Bill came, she had the bottoms leaning against the wall by the back door. The chairs were in their places and the boards from the garage were across two kitchen chairs.

"Sit down at the end of the table there; dinner's about ready," said Mattie.

"This is mighty nice of you, Mrs. Rigsbee." Bill pulled out his chair. "You took the bottoms out already?"

"Oh yes. They're over there by the door."

Bill looked. "I declare Mrs. Rigsbee. You beat all."

"Well, I try to do what I can."

"Something sure smells good. You didn't have to go to all this trouble."

"No trouble. I cook three meals a day. Except for once in a while I'll warm up leftovers—just can't go like I used to. It slips up on you. You'll find out."

"I'm already finding out—I'll tell you." Bill adjusted the board he was sitting on, looked down at it.

"Well," said Mattie, standing at the stove, fork in hand, turning to look at Bill, "I'm lucky to have been able to keep going so long. I thank the Good Lord every day."

"Yeah, well, you sure keep going. That's for sure. Mmmmmm, that smells mighty good."

"Well, it's not much. Alora brought me some corn last Friday and it was too much for one fixing, so I had some left and these potatoes are from Sunday. I picked the tomatoes this morning. I got eight plants. 'Lucky Boys.' But Finner and Alora are mighty good about keeping me stocked with other stuff. No better neighbors in the world. They let me pick all the string beans I want. Alora even helps me; but she ain't careful. She'll pick them too young or too old or with black spots. I took Pearl some. My sister. Told her I was sorry about their condition—but that I'd had help picking them."

"Yeah, Finner and Alora are fine people. That your little dog out there?"

"Lord have mercy, I'm going to have to call the dog-catcher. He just took up. I can't keep a dog." She stirred the potatoes. "This is going to have to warm just a little more."

"He's a right nice little dog."

"He's got possibilities, but I just can't keep up this place and a dog to boot. You want him?"

"Oh no. I got two bird dogs."

Mattie put bowls of food on the table. "Now I want you to eat all you want."

"Good gracious, Mrs. Rigsbee."

"Bow your head and let's say the blessing."

Bill left with the chair bottoms at 12:35. Mattie stacked the dishes beside the sink. She had gotten into the habit of not washing her dishes right away after lunch. She waited until "All My Children" was over at two. Nobody knew.

If anybody ever found out that she both watched that program and didn't clean up right after she ate, she didn't know what she would do.

But after all, things did happen in the real world just like they happened on that program. It *was* all fiction, but anybody who read the paper nowadays knew things like that were happening all the time. And that woman who played the old lady was such a good actress, and Erica, Erica was good, too—such a good character, good actress. People almost exactly like her actually existed all over the place nowadays.

And why shouldn't she sit down for an hour a day after dinner and do something for herself. Why, Alora sat around the house all day watching soap operas and then went so far as to talk to people about them. Alora's watching so much television was one reason that when she went on her daily walk she carried that pistol in her hand under a Kleenex.

Mattie poured gravy over the dog's food and took it out to him. He was standing, waiting. Why, he's already learned to tell time, she thought. I'm going to call the dogcatcher right now.

She put the bowl on the steps and watched him. She had only a few minutes before "All My Children." The dog ate all the food and licked the bowl.

"You're getting a little more frisky, ain't you?" she said. "Well, I ain't able to keep a dog. I'm going in and call the dogcatcher right now." She picked up the bowl, went back inside, looked at the clock on the mantel. It was exactly four minutes until one. "My goodness," she said. She would have time to get through to the dog-catcher—and make it brief. She called from the phone on the counter between the kitchen and den.

A woman answered. Mattie explained about the dog and gave her street address. The woman said the dog-catcher might be by that afternoon, or it could be tomor-row. Mattie hung up and glanced at the clock. It was one o'clock on the dot. She walked into the den, bent over and clicked the TV on. She slowly walked backward, still bending over, toward the rocker. Her left hand reached behind her to find the chair arm. Ah, the commercial— New Blue Cheer—was still on. She had started sitting down when a mental picture flashed into her head: *the chair without a bottom*. But her leg muscles had already gone lax. She was on the way down. Gravity was doing its job. She continued on past the customary stopping place, her eyes fastened to the New Blue Cheer box on the TV screen, her mind screaming no, wondering what bones she might break, wondering how long she was going to keep on going down, down, down.

When she jolted to a stop the backs of her thighs and a spot just below her shoulders were pinched together tightly. Her arms were over her head. Her bottom was one inch from the floor. Nothing hurt except the backs of her legs, and that seemed to be only from the pressure. How *could* she have forgotten? she thought.

She was amazed that her right arm which she normally couldn't lift very high was so high over her head. And not hurting much. She tried to get her arms down but couldn't. She was wedged tightly. What was she going to do? She looked at Erica on the TV screen.

In a straight line were Mattie's eyes, her knees, and Erica's face.

Nothing seemed broken. But her arms were going to go dead to sleep if she didn't hurry and get them down. She needed to pull herself *up* somehow. What in the world? What a ridiculous fix. That dog. If I hadn't been feeding him, she thought, and calling the dogcatcher, this wouldn't have happened. Lord have mercy—what if Alora comes in the back door and sees me watching this program? What in the world will I say? Well, I'll just say I was sitting down to watch the news when I fell through, and so of course I couldn't get up to turn off that silly soap opera. That's what I'll tell her.

Then she will see my dishes stacked over there.

I've *got* to get up. She will know I came over here to sit down before I did my dishes. I've got to . . .

Mattie's predicament suddenly seemed serious. What if . . . Alora might not come. Robert might not come. For sure *he* wouldn't come before Saturday.

Mattie had known all along there was some reason Robert ought to come more than once a week. Well, this proved it. Maybe now he would start coming once in a while to see if she was all right, hadn't had a heart attack, or a stroke, or hadn't . . . for heaven's sake, fallen through a chair. Well, this was the . . . the most ridiculous fix she had ever heard of. If there were some way to get that dog to bark or somehow go get somebody. How in the world could she get that dog to do something?

She needed to get out before that program was over so that, for one thing, if the doorbell rang she could turn the TV off. And if somebody saw her dirty dishes she didn't know how in the world she could explain that.

What if she *died* one day during the hour her dishes were dirty.

She would have to change her routine.

She was looking at the TV. There was that boy who got that girl pregnant. He did it as sure as day and was lying like nobody's business.

Who might come? It was Monday. Bill said he'd bring the chair bottoms back by Thursday. No later than Thursday, he said. Alora or Finner would come over before then, wouldn't they? But what if for some reason they didn't?

She tried to move. Her right arm moved forward and then back. The chair rocked slightly. Well, she was going to have to turn the chair over—or something—to get out, that's all there was to it. Her arm moved back and forth. Then her head, in time with her arm. The chair rocked. Erica was having a conversation with somebody in somebody's foyer. Phillip's. Wasn't his name Phillip?

The phone rang. She couldn't quite see it—over on the kitchen bar. It rang again. She strained to get up somehow; then she gave up. It rang again. Who could it be? Probably Alora. Or Pearl, her sister. It rang again . . . and again. Her rocking stopped. Then the only noise she could hear was the television and the clock ticking on the mantel above her head.

Lamar Benfield had been a dogcatcher for four days. He usually held a job for three, four months, then got tired of it and stopped. But he always saved enough money to keep going until he found another job. And he had a nice shop behind his mobile home—did odd jobs, didn't need an awful lot of money since he was still single.

Lamar liked his new job. He fancied himself as good with animals and had been looking for a job which called for travel and working outside. It was almost dark as he turned into the driveway of a brick ranch house. He had four dogs in back and had decided to get this last one so that his load for tomorrow would be light enough for him to take the afternoon off and change the points and plugs on his pickup.

He rang the front doorbell, adjusted his ball cap, shifted his weight, and looked around for a dog. So far he hadn't been bitten. This he attributed to his way with dogs. He heard something inside. Sounded like a child.

Well, at least somebody was home. Was somebody saying come in? He tried the door. It was locked.

He walked around to the backyard, looked for a dog. There: a fice on the back steps. He wondered if that was the dog he was supposed to pick up. The back door was open. He looked in through the screen, glanced down at the dog. Dog's a little tired or something, he thought. He looked back inside. "Anybody home?"

"Come in. Please come in."

He opened the door and stepped into the den. The room was dark except for the TV and someone sitting . . . Damn, she didn't have no neck at all. That was the littlest person he'd ever . . . Wait a minute. What in the world was . . . ?

It spoke: "I'm stuck in this chair."

His eyes adjusted. She was stuck way down in the frame of a rocking chair. "God Almighty. How long you been like that?" he asked.

"Since the news came on—after lunch. Can you help me get out of here?"

"Well, yes ma'am. I can maybe pull you out."

"Turn on that light. And turn off that television."

The light was bright.

"My Lord," said Mattie, looking up at the dogcatcher. "I'm glad you're here. I was thinking I might have to stay like this all night. Please excuse the mess."

Lamar glanced around. "What mess?"

"Well, I fell through here before I had a chance to do the dishes."

"All right with me. Let's see. Give me your hands and let's see if I can pull you up."

"I don't know."

"Great day, your hands are cold."

Lamar held Mattie's hands and pulled upward. The chair rolled forward on the rockers and then lifted into the air with her still in it. "That ain't going to work," he said, and set her back down.

"Maybe if you can . . ." Mattie couldn't think of a thing to say.

"Let me just look for a minute." Lamar pulled the chair out a little ways and got down on his hands and knees and crawled around the chair. "Hummm," he said, "looks like you're pretty stuck."

"I know it."

"Might have to cut you out."

"Oh no, not this chair. We'll have to figure something else out."

"Well, let's see, as long as, ah . . ."

"Maybe you could turn me over on the side and just push me on through like I was started. Think that would work? I don't want to have to cut this chair."

"Well, I could try. Let's see." Lamar tilted the chair and gently started it to the floor.

"I don't weigh but one ten," said Mattie. "I used to weigh between one thirty and one forty. That's what I weighed all my life until I started falling off."

"You ain't fell off too much."

Mattie lay on the floor, on her side, in the chair.

"You mean," said Lamar, "you want me to just kinda push you on through?"

"Have you got any better ideas?"

"No, I don't guess so. Except cutting you out. Let me

see if I can pull your legs up straight. I'll have to pull your legs up straight before I can push you on through."

The dogs in the truck started barking. The fice barked back.

"You are the dogcatcher, aren't you?"

"Yes ma'am."

"Is that the little fice barking?"

"I think so."

"I never heard him bark."

"Is he the one I come after?"

"He's the one." Mattie gasped, "Oh, that hurt."

"I don't think this is going to work."

"Listen, with all that noise I'm afraid Alora might—Alora's my neighbor—I'm afraid she might come over; I want to ask you if you'd do something for me."

"Okay. Here, let me set you back up." Lamar set Mattie back up.

"Would you wash my dishes?"

"Wash your dishes?"

"It's just a few. If you don't mind. I'll pay you something. I'm just afraid that . . . Would you do it?"

"Now?"

"Yes—if you would."

"Okay." Lamar started to the sink. He stopped and looked back at Mattie. "Would you feel better if I sort of started you rocking or something?"

"No, that's all right. The soap and stuff is all under the sink. Just run some warm water in that far sink and wash them and rinse them and put them in the other sink. The wash rag and drying towel are behind the cabinet door there under the sink."

"I let my dishes sit," said Lamar. "Change the water every three or four days."

Lamar washed the dishes. The dogs were still barking. It was dark outside.

The back floodlights came on at Finner and Alora's. The back of their house faced the back of Mattie's. Finner opened the door and looked out. "What the hell is all that?" he said.

Alora spoke from the kitchen. "Where's all them dogs?"

"In a truck it looks like."

Alora came up behind him. "What in the world? What's going on out there?"

"I reckon it's the dogcatcher. Mattie said she was going to call him, you know."

"You want to walk over there?" asked Alora.

"Naw. I've seen a dogcatcher before."

Lamar finished drying the last dish.

"How about pulling me over there so I can tell you where to put them," said Mattie.

Lamar walked over, took hold of the arms to the rocker and slid Mattie from the den into the kitchen.

"See that cabinet right there?" said Mattie. "No, the one beside it. That's right. The dishes go on the bottom shelf in there. The glasses right above. That's right. Now, put those pans under the sink. Okay. Now just drop the knives and forks in that drawer; no, the one beside it. Okay. Now would you just sort of wipe up there around the sink?"

Lamar cleaned up, then hung the dish rag and towel behind the cabinet door beneath the sink.

"I thank you," said Mattie.

"You're welcome, but we got to get you out of that chair. I think I ought to cut through the back bottom there with a saw or take it apart somehow."

"I don't want you to have to cut it."

"Well, let me see if there's some way I can . . . I could saw it right at the back here and it could be fixed back so you'd never know—glue it and brace it on the inside."

"Well, the saw's hanging in the back of the garage," said Mattie. "I don't know what else to do. Cut the light on there by the door."

Lamar got the saw from the garage, came back, and carefully cut through the bottom back of the chair. He turned Mattie onto her side, and then with Mattie lying on the kitchen floor holding onto the lower ridge of a bottom cabinet door, Lamar pried the rocker apart and pulled it from around her.

Mattie lay on the floor on her side with her knees under her chin. She tried to straighten out.

"Let me help you up," said Lamar. He placed his hands under her arms and lifted her. Mattie remained bent.

"Set me on the couch," she said.

Lamar shuffled with her over to the couch and set her down.

"My Lord," she said. "What a predicament. I have never in my life. What do I owe you?"

"Not a thing. I've just got to get the dog and get going."

"Well, let me feed him." Mattie stood very slowly. She

was bent. Lamar reached for her. She kept one hand on the arm of the couch.

"I can make it; just a little stiff. If I take my time I'll straighten out. My Lord. Wait a minute. Let me kind of shake my arms a minute here."

Severely humped, so that she had to look up toward her eyebrows to see straight ahead, Mattie walked slowly by Lamar, into the kitchen, and opened the refrigerator door. She got out a plate of chicken and a bowl of congealed gravy. With a fork she raked the meat off a chicken leg and thigh into a small pan. She spooned on gravy, then poured it all over two open biscuits in the dog's bowl. Bent over, holding the bowl, she walked to Lamar. "Would you feed him that before you take him?" she said.

Lamar took the bowl. "I guess so. If I got time. I got to get on back."

"He's hungry. He ain't eat since one."

Lamar started out the back door.

"Let it cool a little before you put it down," said Mattie.

Lamar fed the dog, then took him away.

That night, after a long hot bath, Mattie noticed that her back, arm, and leg muscles felt weak—she knew they would be sore in the morning.

She sat at her piano in the living room. On top of the piano was a picture of Paul, her husband, who had died five years earlier; a picture of Robert; one of Elaine, now thirty-eight, unmarried, a twelfth-grade English teacher—gifted and talented; and a picture of the entire family together. The piano was a black studio Wurlitzer—one she and Paul had bought for Robert and Elaine. Robert had taken lessons for two years and quit. Elaine had taken for four. But she, Mattie, played just about every night, sitting on the bench stuffed with old hymnbooks, thumbing through the Broadman Hymnal until she found one of the fifteen or twenty hymns she played well. She could read hymns in the easier keys, playing partly by ear.

She played "What a Friend We Have in Jesus," "Blessed Assurance," and "Send the Light." No damage to her arms from the chair accident, she decided. Then she played "To a Wild Rose," not a hymn. She had listened as Elaine learned it years ago and liked it so much she learned it herself, and now played it almost every night.

As she walked to her bedroom, more stiffly than normal, she thought about the little dog. "I'm too old to keep a dog," she said.

II

Tuesday morning Mattie lay in bed on her back, awake. She turned onto her side, pushed up, swung her legs to the floor, stood, straightened, and raised her arms as high as she could, not very high.

Well, nothing was broken. No sharp pains. But she was sore. She was sure sore. The backs of her legs especially. She walked over to her dresser mirror, pulled her pajama bottoms down to her knees and turned around so she could see the backs of her legs. They were bruised badly. How about that. Wasn't that the most ridiculous thing in the world?

Now, who in the world can I tell? she thought. Well, nobody. That was such a ridiculous thing to do. But it was funny, too. She sat back down on the edge of the bed, looked at Paul's picture on the wall. He would have wanted to keep it a secret. Paul would have been very embarrassed about the whole affair.

She saw herself starting down backwards toward the open chair. She saw her butt going down into the open hole. She smiled, then laughed out loud, stopped the laugh with her hand over her mouth, laughed again. She saw herself crunched down in the rocking chair, her feet straight up. She laughed again, her knotted hands spread behind her on the bed, her head back. She kept laughing, fell back on the bed laughing, held her stomach, laughing. She would have to tell Pearl, her sister. It was so funny. But nobody else. Oh, she was sure sore.

The phone on her bedside table rang.

She turned onto her side, sobered, pushed herself up, and answered.

It was Lamar, the dogcatcher. "Mrs. Rigsbee, you seen my billfold?"

"No. But I haven't been in the kitchen or out in the backyard. I just got up. You're up mighty early."

"Yeah, they called me about this pack of dogs north of town. My billfold fell out of my pocket sometime and the only time I can figure is maybe when I was on the floor there at your house."

"Wait a minute. I'll go look." Mattie, her legs and back sore, walked along the narrow carpeted hall and into the den. She was barefooted, wearing the pink pajamas that Elaine gave her and made her promise to wear because Mattie had been sleeping in just her underwear. Pearl also insisted she wear the pajamas. What if you died in your sleep in just your underwear? Pearl had said.

There it was. A black billfold lying on the floor right there beside the big armchair, next to the rocker. She picked it up and took it over to the kitchen phone.

"It's right here. Was right here on the floor. I'll keep it for you."

"Thanks. I'll be by afterwhile."

"I'm a little sore this morning."

"I guess you are."

"But thank goodness nothing's broke. Listen, you come on at about 11:30 and I'll have you a little bite to eat."

"Well . . . I got to, ah . . . I got to be out that way. Maybe I could. What you going to have?"

"'What am I going to *have?*' 'I don't like butter, is your meat lean?'"

"What?"

"It's a saying. What Sukie Smith said one time. She was picky. We always remembered it. If you want something to eat you come on around 11:30; I'll have something either way."

"Okay, maybe I will."

"Well, you come on. Bye."

"Bye."

I bet he comes, thought Mattie. She looked at his billfold, beside the phone. Thick, heavy looking. She shouldn't look in it. She wouldn't.

Let's see, she thought, I got soup, vegetables. I ought to cook a little something extra. I got them potatoes. Potato salad. I hadn't done any potato salad in I don't know when. And I can make that hamburger into a meatloaf easy enough.

She walked back down the hall, put on her green housecoat, her slippers, and sweater, put the bedroom phone back on the hook, walked back to the kitchen, lifted the cast-iron frying pan from beneath the sink, got bacon from the refrigerator, pulled out three slices, separated them, carefully placed them into the pan, cut the eye on, struck a match, stuck it under the pan, cut the flame back, and got out the eggs. Cook the bacon slow, starting in a cold pan.

After breakfast, she put on the water to boil, peeled, cut potatoes, dropped them into the water. She wasn't going to be overcome by a little soreness. Alora would do a little something to her foot, say, and there she'd be sitting with it propped up—days at a time. Overcome. Mattie was not that way. If something was sore, she kept it moving to get the soreness out. Nobody in her family— unless they'd married in—had ever stayed still for anything to get well. Course a lot of them were dead now too, but not from just sitting. Some had died young— when that wasn't so unusual. She and Pearl were the only two left.

When the potato salad was all ready she looked in the cabinet for paprika. She always liked to sprinkle a little paprika on her potato salad for color. Tasted good, too. Ah, there it was.

She sprinkled.

That stuff's turned a little dark, I believe. It's sure turned a little dark. I didn't know I'd had it in there that long. What in the world? Let's see what it tastes like.

Hot . . . What . . . ? *Chili powder!*

My goodness to gracious.

Mattie found a spoon, scraped away the chili powder, and found the paprika.

Have mercy. She would tell Pearl. Pearl would die laughing. She would tell Pearl—tell her that first and then about the chair.

Mattie thought about the chair. She started laughing again. She put both hands on the counter at the sink and, laughing, looked out through the window into her backyard. She felt the soreness in the backs of her legs, in her back, and shoulders, as she laughed out loud. She laughed harder as she saw herself, feet and arms straight up, rear end all the way down to the floor, stuck. She thought of the Emmett Leftcourt story that Pearl's husband Carl used to tell about how Emmett started out as a police officer, then got to fishing and drinking so much and started going down and quit his job and started waiting tables at the Conventional Cafe at Mattamuskeet, fishing and drinking all the time, and then got fired and kept on going downhill. Carl would tell it, embellish it, about how Emmett got fired and moved in with the old catfishers who lived in a rusted tin-roof shack made from drink cartons and scrap wood. They caught and sold catfish until they had enough money for whiskey. Carl followed Emmett Leftcourt's career, watching him go on downhill, and one day walked by the shack and of all things out there in the front yard Emmett and another man were boiling a sea heron, his long stick-legs sticking straight up out of the pot, and Carl would get so tickled telling this, holding his arms straight up like the heron legs, and then when you thought he was through, Carl would say that a few weeks later a stumbling, dirty, old drunk man walked up to him and—standing still but sort of stumbling, looking down and then up into Carl's eyes—said, "Do you know Emmett Leftcourt?" and Carl said yes and the old drunk said, "You know, he's one of the sorriest men I ever met."

Pearl would try to tell it but never got it as good as Carl. Mattie thought about the sea heron's legs sticking up out of that pot, about herself in the chair. She laughed again, looked down at the billfold.

She picked it up and opened it. There was a twenty-dollar bill and a folded-up something—letter? Stuck in there where the money goes, a folded letter or something on yellow lined notebook paper.

The food was all on the stove; it was 11:00 A.M. He'd probably be by pretty soon. She would see what the yellow paper was. Nobody would ever know. And it wouldn't hurt one thing in the world. He was liable to come in ten minutes or so and if she didn't look now she'd never as long as she lived know whether or not it was a love letter, or what.

DEAR LAMAR:

I want you to try to get me out of here If you can sign this thing they'll put me in your Custody Some of the people here are real Shits They will put us in a solatary confinment room if we mess up. They done had me in there twice and I didn't do a thing. How are You doing these days, fine I hope. Lamar, all you have to do is sign this paper. If I got a legal guiardan everything will be fine Ok? You can tell them I'm going to live with you, then there wont be no more trouble for me.

SINCERLY YOURS,
WESLEY.

Such language, thought Mattie. The back doorbell rang. A wave of panic swept over her, hurting the backs of her legs. She folded the letter quickly, stuck it back into the billfold. "Come on in."

Alora came in the back door. Mattie noticed that Alora's hair had been freshly dyed black. It would look so much better natural, she thought, and she wondered why Alora didn't either lose weight or buy larger pants suits.

Lord, I hope she don't stay long, thought Mattie. I got to tend my food.

"I thought I'd come over and see about the dog. They got him didn't they?" Alora was eating an apple.

"Sure did. I can't keep a dog with all I got to do around this place. And I got the Lottie Moon coming up, starting early again. I reckon they'll ask me again this year. Lord, I wouldn't have kept that dog a minute a year ago. I must be going soft."

"Yeah, we heard the dogcatcher over here last night." Alora stepped on over into the kitchen. "I reckon the little thing's dead by now," she said. "Gassed, I imagine."

"I don't know. Sit down over here at the table. I got to tend to my food a little bit. Watch out! Not that one. The bottom's out. Sit on the one there with the board."

Alora looked at the chair. "You got your seats out?"

"Yeah, I wanted some of that oil cloth stuff you can

wipe off easy. I don't even think they make real oil cloth anymore. You know, sort of like you got."

"Yeah. It does make it lots easier—you can just wipe them right off." Alora needed to throw away her apple core. She walked to the trash can where on top of a wadded-up piece of paper she saw the handful of sawdust Mattie had swept up from the kitchen floor the night before. "What you been cutting?"

"What?"

"What you been cutting? This sawdust."

"Oh that. The sawdust. I just, ah, cut a board."

"What kind of board?"

"Just a board. To ah, to put over my chairs there."

The back doorbell rang. It was the dogcatcher.

"Come on in." Mattie stepped toward the door as he came in. "This is Alora Swanson, my next-door neighbor. And—you know I don't believe I got your name."

"Lamar. Lamar Benfield. Nice to meet you," he said to Alora.

"Here's your billfold." Mattie handed it to him. "Lamar was by for the dog yesterday," Mattie said to Alora, "and his billfold dropped out of his pocket."

"While I was down on the floor sawing the chair I guess," said Lamar.

"What chair?" said Alora.

"That one over there. The one Mrs., ah, she got hung in."

Alora looked over at the chair. "Hung in? Mattie? You sat in that, without the *bottom* in it?"

"I sure did." Mattie laughed a short burst. "Ain't that something."

"Well, I'll say it is. You just sat down there and got stuck?"

"That's right. I hadn't planned on telling anybody. It was so silly."

Alora laughed. "Well, Mattie, I declare." She laughed again. "And you're okay?"

"I'm okay. Sit down over there, Lamar," said Mattie, pointing toward the couch. Now the whole neighborhood and everybody at church will know, she thought. It *was* funny, but Pearl was enough to know about that. She walked over, looked at her beans and cut back the heat. When in the world is Alora going home?

"So you're the dogcatcher?" said Alora, walking into the den.

"That's right. That's right."

"I don't think I ever met a dogcatcher."

"Well, it's a job," said Lamar, swiping at his nose with the back of his index finger.

I wish he would take his hat off, thought Mattie. Young men, nowadays. Ball hats. Nobody to teach them anything I guess. Why Paul would of no more wore a hat in the house than he would of . . . wore a snake. I wish Alora would go on home.

Alora looked over her shoulder. "That sure smells good," she said.

"Why don't you stay and eat a bite?"

"No. I'm trying to get Finner's socks sewed up. He wears them work shoes, hard as iron in the back or something, and he wears holes in the heels in no time at all. Mainly his left one for some reason."

I wish she would go on home so I could feed this young

man his dinner. It's 11:30 and I want him out of here by one. "You know you can get socks with the heel reinforced. At Sears."

"That's what I'll do, buy some at Sears. Well, listen, I got to get going. Finner'll be home in a few minutes and I got to put together a little something for us to eat."

Well leave then, thought Mattie.

Alora placed her hand on the screen-door handle. "Are you from around here?" she asked Lamar.

"Yeah. I'm from between here and Prosser Hills."

"Well, you're 'hometown,' ain't you?"

"I reckon I am."

"Mattie, you take care now. Don't overdo after your fall."

"I won't."

Alora left.

"This'll all be ready in just a minute," said Mattie. Who was that Wesley? Mattie thought. It had slipped her mind, blurred—was Lamar a brother, uncle? Didn't the letter say uncle. His brother's boy. Could be his sister's boy. Well, Lamar was nice enough looking, if he'd fix himself up a little bit. If he'd just take that hat off. If he wore it to the table she'd take it off his head and hang it up. She couldn't sit through a meal with a man with a hat on his head. Young people nowadays just didn't—

Lamar stood, walked to the rocker and inspected it where it was cut through. "I could fix this for you if you want me to. I got a little shop out behind my house. I could glue this thing, brace and bolt it on the inside here, and it'd be like new."

"Well, I don't know. Bill Yeats does most of my furniture work if I ever have any. Covering stuff and things."

"I'll give you a good deal. I'm thinking about getting into the furniture business full time. Mostly repair and stuff."

"Maybe so." Mattie set pots of food on the table, on coasters, little wood coasters that Elaine had made in Bible school thirty years ago. She went back to the stove and stirred the soup. If Elaine would get married, Mattie thought, she could have some children who could make coasters to replace these, and her grandchildren could make some to replace those—on down the line. And then there was Mattie's button collection in the big jar, the collection her great-grandmother Ella started, the one Mattie had kept and added to; Elaine would probably end up with it and then if she didn't have any children, there'd come a time when those buttons wouldn't get a one added, and they'd end up no telling where, in a shop where not a soul had the slightest idea where those buttons came from, what all they'd seen and lived through, starting out before her great-grandmother, that jar of buttons that she'd played with when she was a little girl, the jar that always had a matchup for somebody's lost button; there'd be nobody to add the first button—nobody who knew what they were dealing with. Those buttons scattered to the four winds and nobody knowing, caring where they came from. "Come on over and have a seat. Everything's ready."

Lamar walked over. He wore heavy construction shoes, blue jeans, a plaid shirt, and his red "Red Man" cap.

"Sit right there on the board," said Mattie. "I don't want to have to cut *you* out. I just got to fix the tea. Here, let me hang your hat up." Mattie grabbed the bill of Lamar's hat. She remembered that he'd had it on the night before—suddenly realized he might be bald. Together they pulled the hat from his head. A full shock of curly brown hair was freed. "Let me hang this up on the hall rack."

For lunch Lamar usually had two wrapped grocery-store ham and cheeses and a Mello Yello; or a Big Mac, fries, Coke, apple turnover, or if he had time, a Personal Pan Pizza at Pizza Hut. And at night at home alone he usually had crackers, Vienna sausages or sardines, a small can of peaches, and a six-pack of Miller. When he got low on money he cut back on the beer.

Lamar looked at the food. What a spread. Hot food. Vegetables all over the place. Soup—thick vegetable soup. Three kinds of pickles, chow-chow. Fresh tomatoes. He tried growing three tomato plants once, but they died in spite of the fact he put fertilizer on them every morning at 7:30.

"Let's say the blessing," said Mattie, bowing her head.

Lamar looked at her.

"Dear God, bless this food to the nourishment of our bodies."

Lamar bowed his head.

"In Thy precious name. Amen."

The phone rang. Mattie answered.

It was Alora. "Mattie, I'm watching out over there. Finner and me are worried about that dogcatcher. I'll call back in thirty minutes or so. You don't never know with all that's going on these days. Say 'yes' or something so he won't suspect."

"Ah . . . well, yes."

"He's liable to hit you in the head and take all your money."

"No. I don't think so."

"Don't let on. You just can't tell these days. We'll keep a watch out. I might send Finner over to sit by your back door."

"That's okay. I don't think there's any need—" she looked at Lamar who was holding and looking at his bitten-into-once piece of cornbread, turning it over in his hand while he chewed—"any need to do that."

"Don't let on it was me. And if anything happens, throw something through your kitchen screen or fall out the back door, or scream. We're going to eat out in the backyard so it won't be no trouble for us to watch."

"Well, okay. Bye-bye."

Mattie hung up. That Alora. Sometimes . . . Lamar was helping himself to the peas. She stood at the table. "That was Alora. About one of her children. No better neighbors in the world. Her and Finner Swanson. Finner was a delivery man for Hostess. He's retired. You might have run into him sometime on your rounds."

"No, not any Hostess," said Lamar, his mouth full.

"Let's see." Mattie looked to the stove to see what else there was to do. "Oh, the tea. I forgot the tea." She put ice in two glasses, cut a lemon, squeezed and dropped in lemon slices, poured tea, and set the glasses on the table. "Get all the cornbread you want," she said, sitting down at the table. Lamar took another piece. "And try some of those pickles."

Lamar stuck a pickle with his fork.

Finner, then Alora, started down their back steps. Holding their glasses of iced tea and plates of Stouffer's Lasagna which Alora had mixed with extra cheddar cheese and hamburger, they kept their eyes on Mattie's house while they slowly felt their way down the steps with their feet.

"You got any kinfolks around?" Mattie asked.

"Oh yeah, couple of uncles and stuff. And I got a nephew in the YMRC for stealing a car. Except I ain't but eight years older than him."

"Is that right? His mama and daddy must be pretty upset."

"Naw, they ain't upset."

"Where do they live?"

"Can you pass me just a little more of that?"

Mattie passed the potato salad.

"They're in—well, I don't really know where his mama is. She started out illegitimate. At least that's what she used to say. Wilma Turner was her name. Wesley's daddy is my brother, Milton, and he lives in Phoenix." Lamar took a swallow of tea.

Mattie waited for him to continue. "Arizona," she said.

"Yeah, Arizona."

"Did they just leave him?"

"Well, they got married when they were eighteen—in Dillon, South Carolina, and stayed there. Wilma stole some money from this restuarant where she was a waitress so they could get married and then they changed their names so it turned out they didn't exist or something."

"And so he was born down there?"

There was a knock at the back door. It was Finner. "Mattie," he called through the screen.

Mattie got up.

"Alora sent me over for a cup of sugar. You doing all right?"

"I'm doing fine."

"Here's a cup."

Mattie poured Finner a cup of sugar and handed it out the back door. She sat back down at the table. "So he got born down there?"

"It was pretty much a mix-up. This is sure good food."

"Thank you. What got mixed up?"

"Milton came home from South Carolina with this baby, Wesley, and put him in the Berry Hill Orphanage and didn't tell anybody—gave him his mama's last name which didn't exist because of the name mix-up or something, and Wesley didn't get his real name back until they put him in the YMRC. But see, the problem was Milton put *my* name on some form, told them *he* was Wesley's uncle, then moved to Phoenix. Mama and Daddy wouldn't ever believe none of it 'cause they never saw Wesley in the first place and I'm the one that would get these official letters and stuff from the orphanage."

"Here, let me get you a little more tea. Well, I declare, idn't that something. Do you ever go see him?"

"Yeah, I go see him every once in a while. He writes me letters. He left the orphanage and stole this car and they put him in the YMRC."

Mattie tried to visualize Wesley in the Young Men's Rehabilitation Center.

III

When Lamar left, he took the rocker with him. He told Mattie he'd bring it back Saturday morning. *Late* morning, he was thinking, so maybe he could eat lunch with her.

"That'll be fine," said Mattie. "You come about noon and I'll have you a bite to eat," she said, following Lamar out into the yard.

Back inside, she turned on "All My Children," and walked over to the kitchen sink. It just went to show you—this Wesley business—that we are closer to real crime than we think. It's in our families nowadays, all around us with the way people are forgetting God. Mattie watched and listened to the program as she cleaned her dishes—she would try both at the same time for a while. Sometimes the program was a little embarrassing, but it was the real world. She remembered how the world used to be so much less complicated. There was your family, there were friends, and there were criminals. They never got mixed together. Now you just never knew. But she wasn't going to go crazy over it all like Alora, Alora *and* Finner—Finner sleeping with a gun under his pillow.

After the program, Mattie decided it was time to call her sister Pearl, and tell her about falling through the chair. Pearl was two years older than Mattie and had stopped going to Listre Baptist the month the church carpeted the backs of the pews, hung microphones over the choir, and started busing. She said it was all a waste of money, and tacky to boot.

Pearl laughed about the rocking chair, and said it was a wonder Mattie hadn't broke a bone.

They talked for twenty minutes. When Mattie was about to hang up, Pearl asked her if she was still planning to go with her up to the funeral home so they could each pick out a casket. With all the excitement Mattie had forgotten.

"Lord, I forgot. I guess it's really not such a bad idea, but . . ."

"I'll come on by. I told them we'd be there at four. It'll be good to get it all off your mind."

"I ain't had it on my mind."

"Well, it wouldn't be a bad idea. They're real good about it. Hanna Brown went, and Mr. Crosley, you know, works up there, was real nice. They serve you coffee and everything. Chocolate cake. You can at least see what they got even if you don't pick out one right yet."

"Well . . . What are you going to wear?"

"I thought I'd dress up."

"Come on by. I'll see what I can find to wear." Mattie decided not to take a bath. Instead she'd apply some fresh underarm deodorant. She used baking soda, with just enough water to make a little paste.

Pearl opened the back screen and came in. She favored Mattie, but was older, shorter, and wider than Mattie. She looked like an old, wise, white-haired Indian chief, solid, shaped like a square with far-apart legs which seemed to start toward each other just above the ankles. She wore a plain print dress, pearls, and held her black pocketbook under her arm. When she walked she swayed far to the right, then far to the left. She wouldn't use a cane. Mattie hoped she'd start using one before she just toppled over on her side one day.

Pearl sat down on the couch, sighed, snapped open her purse, pulled out a small tin of snuff. She opened the tin, pinched some snuff between her fingers, and placed it inside her lower lip. She replaced the tin top, put the tin back in her purse, and fished around in there until she found her clean McCormick dill-seed jar and set it on the couch beside her. She snapped her purse back shut. "Well, show me how you fell through the rocking chair."

Mattie told Pearl all about what happened; she left out "All My Children." Pearl knew she watched it and Mattie knew Pearl knew, but it was not discussed just as Pearl's snuff was not discussed.

In telling the story, Mattie acted out her movements back from the television. Pearl started laughing. Mattie kept telling. Pearl laughed louder. Mattie talked louder and got to laughing herself. They were both laughing—hard. Pearl pulled a Kleenex from her purse.

Mattie told about how she heard the clock strike one, one-thirty, two, two-thirty, and on and on; how she watched all those programs; how she saw the dogcatcher through the closed storm door, standing there on the front porch waiting for her to come. How he came in the back door, washed her dishes directly, and finally sawed her out of her chair.

"I don't think I've heard of such a thing," said Pearl, "since Alfred or some of them tied little Durk's foot to the fence that time."

"I remember that," said Mattie. She laughed. "Poor little Durk. They picked on him all the time."

Pearl capped her dill-seed jar and put it inside her pocketbook. "Well I guess we ought to get started. I told them four. I need to go to the bathroom before we leave." Pearl stood and walked to the bathroom. When she returned, she asked Mattie, "How come your toilet seat so sticky?"

"I don't know unless I . . ."

"I wiped it off. It was just as sticky as I don't know what."

"Well, I . . . Lord, I guess I washed it with Listerine."

"Listerine!"

"About a month ago I used Listerine instead of alcohol—got them confused—and so I guess I did it again. I declare."

They laughed.

"Wait'll I tell Alora," said Pearl.

"Don't tell Alora; it'll get to Myrtle and then everybody in the Sunday school will know; then everybody in the church will know. I know they'll all find out about the chair. And I hadn't planned to tell anybody but you."

"Well, let's go. I'll drive," said Pearl. "We'll get up there about ten minutes early. Mr. Crosley'll meet us. He knows we're coming."

"Don't get me tickled."

"I won't. Don't you get me tickled."

"I'm plenty sore," said Mattie as they got into the car.

Mr. Crosley was waiting for them in the funeral home lobby. He spoke softly, with a slight rasp in his voice, "Mrs. Turnage, Mrs. Rigsbee? How are y'all today?"

"Fine."

"Just fine. How are you, Mr. Crosley?"

"Just dandy. Idn't it a nice day out there? That little cool breeze."

"It sure is."

"Yes, it is."

"You-all follow me right on up the stairs here and let's get you a little cup of coffee before we do anything else. Maybe a little piece of chocolate cake."

Mr. Crosley started up the stairs.

"Wait a minute," said Pearl. "Let me look here at the roster, see who's up here. I might know one." She looked at the names. "No . . ."

"Let me see," said Mattie.

Mr. Crosley waited at the foot of the stairs and then as Pearl and Mattie came along, he started up ahead of them.

Pearl, under her breath, said, "I want a *big* piece of chocolate cake."

"Me too," Mattie mouthed silently.

Mr. Crosley stopped and turned on the stairs. "You all do drink coffee, don't you?" he asked.

"Oh, yes."

"We got some soft drinks too."

Upstairs, they walked along a carpeted hall and into a small kitchen area with a round table, a sink, a Mr. Coffee, and refrigerator. On the table were two pieces of chocolate cake, two coffee cups, cream, sugar, and two navy blue cloth napkins. "Here we go," said Mr. Crosley, pulling out a chair for Pearl.

As she started to sit, Pearl said, "I'm thinking about getting something in a plaid." She cut her eyes to Mattie.

"Beg your pardon?" said Mr. Crosley, leaning his head forward.

"Pearl!" said Mattie.

"Just kidding." Pearl laughed softly.

"Oh, you want something in a *plaid*," said Mr. Crosley. "Ah, ha. Well, I'm not so sure we've got anything in stock." He slipped the chair under Pearl and bent over her shoulder, "but I imagine we could order something."

"Let's drink a cup of coffee first," said Mattie.

Mr. Crosley took their cups, stepped over to the coffee maker and poured coffee. "Well, you ladies make yourself at home, and I'll be right back." He set the cups of coffee on the table. "I need to go get our brochure and a few other things which will help me explain exactly how we believe we can help you."

Mattie and Pearl ate cake and sipped coffee.

"This is a right nice little kitchen," said Mattie. "This is cake mix, though—bought."

"What you expect in a funeral home? They stay busy doing other things. You know, I remember coming up here when Carl died."

"Well, I guess this is all good. It keeps Robert and Elaine from having to do it all for me."

"I don't know who would do it for me if I didn't."

"Pearl. There are plenty of people. Me."

"I'm not sure you'd get the color right."

"I probably wouldn't." Mattie took a bite of cake. "Well, you know, I hadn't thought about it but I would like to know what I'd be wearing so I could get a match," said Mattie.

"You ought to decide. I got mine hung in the closet and labeled."

"Labeled? What in the world does it say?"

"'Funeral.'"

"I declare, Pearl. You hadn't ever told me that. What is it?"

"That sort of cream pink suit and a white blouse. I just did it a few weeks ago. I'm thinking about buying another suit just like it so I can wear it every once in a while." She took a bite of cake. "I don't have anybody to take care of all that. I got to thinking about it. Besides, I always say, 'Dying is part of living.' I believe it, too. And I'm going to have my funeral at the Free Will where they've just got plain wood inside."

Mr. Crosley came back in with folders and brochures. "Let me show you ladies what we can do for you. How was that cake?"

"Good," said Mattie. "Real good."

"We got more if you want it." Mr. Crosley smiled, sat down, tapped the ends of the folders on the table. "Okay, here's the basic set-up, if I can just show you here in this brochure. Basically, what we do is provide all services, including any details you want to indicate, at today's cost. That's the plan I recommend. We will be able to guarantee you—if you pay now—the same services at any time in the future with no added costs. As you see here, you can indicate the number of cars you think might be needed for the family and such as that. By the way, I can't remember ever having so much fun as I had with you-all in that car at Miss, ah, who was it?—Miss Hattie's funeral. Your cousin. I just . . . you know, it won't in bad taste in the least. It's just that most folks—"

"Well, since she was just a cousin," said Pearl, "it didn't seem quite so sad to us."

"She didn't have nothing *but* cousins," said Mattie.

"No, I don't think she did," said Pearl.

"That's a fact. She didn't," said Mr. Crosley. "But, anyway. I know I've never had as much fun on the job. Who was that other woman?"

"Alora. Alora Swanson, my neighbor," said Mattie.

"She was just along for the ride," said Pearl.

"Just along for the *ride*?" said Mr. Crosley. "Oh, me." He laughed. "Just along for the ride. Well, let's get back to our brochure here."

"Let me use your bathroom first," said Pearl, standing.

"Out and to the left, first door on the right; can't miss it."

Mattie knew Pearl would take a fresh dip of snuff to help settle her nerves.

Mr. Crosley poured Mattie more coffee.

When Pearl came back in, she said, "I kinda want to see the caskets," she said. "Could we do that now? Then talk all about the arrangements?"

"Oh yes, oh yes," said Mr. Crosley. "Right this way. Right this way."

Mattie was immediately struck by a light gray casket there against the far wall. "I see the one I want," she said.

Pearl punched her. "Wait 'til you find out about the costs," she whispered. She pointed to one near them with a head-to-foot lid raised. "Look," she said. "There's a convertible."

"Bless my soul," said Mr. Crosley. "I never heard it called that." He laughed. "I need you two up here all the time."

Mr. Crosley's back was to Pearl. She pulled up her dill-seed jar from her pocketbook, spit, and placed the jar back inside her pocketbook: three seconds. The dill-seed jar was wedged in a corner of her pocketbook, uncapped, held upright with five full Kleenex travel packs.

"Let me show you this one first," said Mr. Crosley. "Actually we have three here which are very similar. Of course, we're working our way around to the more expensive models—here, right here behind us, the oak—pure oak."

"They *are* beautiful," said Mattie. "Look at that finish. How much is that one?"

"This model—the dark one—is a little more than four thousand."

"Gosh," said Mattie. "I'd forgot they were that much."

"That's about what I expected," said Pearl, "for the nicer ones. How heavy is one?" she asked.

"This is on rollers," said Mr. Crosley, touching one of the cheaper models. "Push it if you want to. To get an idea."

Pearl set her pocketbook behind her on the oak casket—at the head, on the wood ledge above the white satin pillow. As she pushed to test the weight of the other casket, Mattie's elbow toppled the pocketbook over onto the pillow. None of them saw it fall.

"That's pretty heavy," said Pearl. "Are they all that heavy? My pallbearers ain't going to be all that sprightly."

"Approximately the same weight. All very sturdily made. Now, as we go around in this direction, the models will get a bit more expensive."

Pearl couldn't remember where she left her purse. She looked around, didn't see it anywhere. Mattie and Mr. Crosley were moving on ahead. She'd been right over . . . She stepped toward the oak casket. Lord have mercy. *Lord have mercy.* The dill seed jar had slid right out onto the pillow and . . . Mr. Crosley and Mattie were moving on, Mr. Crosley talking. Pearl quickly picked up her pocketbook and the dill seed jar. Not one bit had gotten on her pocketbook. But that white satin pillow. She looked up—Mattie's and Mr. Crosley's backs were to her.

She turned the pillow over, patted it once and moved on. Whoever used it wouldn't care.

Pearl caught up. Mr. Crosley was talking. "This color is very nice. Oh, by the way, I forgot. I should tell you that we're getting in several models of stainless steels one day next week probably."

"Stainless steel?" said Mattie. She turned around and looked at Pearl. "Did you hear that? Stainless steel. Maybe we should come back."

"Well . . . I don't know. You really think so?"

"I don't want to make a decision without seeing the stainless steels," said Mattie. "Would it be all right if we came back?" she said to Mr. Crosley.

"Why certainly. No problem at all. I'll give one of you a call when they come in, Mrs. Turnage."

"What's the advantage of the stainless steel?" asked Pearl.

"It lasts," said Mr. Crosley.

"Oh, I see."

"Although I don't think you're going to find anything more beautiful than the oak," said Mr. Crosley.

"You ought to buy one then," said Mattie. "Get on the plan yourself."

That night Mattie watched a show about alligators. She enjoyed the nature programs more than any others except Billy Graham. Sometimes she called Robert or Elaine when an especially good nature program was coming on. And she always called to remind them when Billy Graham was coming on, but later if she asked them if they watched it, they hadn't.

Before going to bed Mattie played "Love Lifted Me," "When I Survey the Wondrous Cross," and "To a Wild Rose." She hummed "Walking Across Egypt," that hymn her father used to sing to her. She couldn't remember the words. She had the music to it somewhere. And he'd used that title as a saying all the time. He had sung a different song for each child before bedtime, and sometimes he sung to them in the daytime during a water break in the fields. He died from typhoid fever when she was eight, Pearl was ten, four older brothers, and one on the way.

On Thursday afternoon, Bill Yeats brought back the covered chair bottoms. He arrived at about 3:30. Mattie had a pound cake, apple pie, and vanilla ice cream for him to choose from.

Before Bill ate, he screwed in the four kitchen-chair bottoms. He leaned the rocker-chair bottom against the wall in the den. "Where's your rocker?"

"Dogcatcher's got it. I had a little accident with it. Set through it without the bottom in it. And the dogcatcher had to cut me out. He's putting it back together where he sawed it."

"Good gracious. You hurt yourself?"

"Oh, no."

Bill chose apple pie and ice cream.

As Mattie cut the pie and then dipped ice cream she studied the color of the kitchen-chair bottoms. She put the pie and ice cream in front of Bill. "Let me just look over here a minute." She walked over and inspected the rocker bottom. Come to think of it, the color that was on them before was just right. "They're too yellow, I think," she said. "I know you think I'm crazy, but I'll tell you what I was thinking; do you still have that material that was on them?"

"It's around the shop somewhere."

"Well, if you could get it cleaned and put it back on and cover them with clear plastic I'd be much obliged. Do you have any clear plastic?"

"Oh yes."

"I just know I'd be happy with that. I'll pay you, of course."

"No problem, no problem at all, Mrs. Rigsbee. I'll just take them right back."

"Well, I sure do appreciate it."

When Bill finished his ice cream and pie, he unscrewed the bottoms, and as he left said, "If this keeps up, Mrs. Rigsbee, I'm going to gain ten, fifteen pounds."

"Wouldn't hurt none. You could use a little filling out."

Later, Mattie walked out to the garage and found boards to cover her remaining three open chair bottoms. No need not to have your kitchen like you want it if that's where you spend most of your life, she thought, and course that's changing some, with me slowing down and all. But I can't like it in here with chair bottoms that are too yellow. It needs to be comfortable. I might as well do a little something for myself once in a while. And the least I can do is leave things the right color. Course Robert's liable to sell them. No telling what he might do. Maybe I should leave them to Elaine and . . . I do have to get all that straight in the will like Alora said.

*   *   *

Robert called Friday and said he was coming for lunch on Saturday. Mattie was glad because she wanted to talk to him about about her will, about who was to get what. No need not to talk about it, think about it. Everybody had to die sooner or later. You might as well face it.

That dogcatcher was supposed to come too, and bring back her rocker. She wondered what Robert would think of him.

Robert showed up early, at about eleven, while Mattie was in the garden picking tomatoes. The food was on: string beans, corn and butterbeans, chicken, creamed potatoes, cornbread, and some good early bitter turnip salet. Robert went in, not noticing Mattie in the garden. He stood at the desk in the den and looked through the mail. He was on several mailing lists that still had his old address. He walked past the counter over to the stove and picked up the lids to each pot to see what was cooking.

Mattie came in with a wicker basket full of tomatoes. "Howdy. I don't know how I got so behind on tomatoes."

Mattie had always hoped Robert would grow up to be a doctor or preacher and that Elaine would marry one. But Robert was an unmarried businessman and Elaine, an unmarried teacher, and every week the chances for grandchildren grew slimmer.

They both dated. Dated fairly nice people. For almost a year, Elaine had dated a "farm worker" who Mattie thought would be a *farm worker*, but he was from Boston, and worked for the state. Something about crops. He went on crop walks—looking at crops. And Robert had dated three different supermarket check-out girls. One had been very young. But neither Robert nor Elaine had ever dated the same person over a year or so, and then three years ago Elaine had said she wanted to not date at all for a while so she could get to know herself. Mattie argued with her that she ought to already know herself—after thirty-five years. Elaine angrily said that well, she didn't, so Mattie backed off. Mattie had always dreamed of their talking together as Elaine grew older, about woman things. There would be so much to talk about. But it never happened that way. It always seemed like maybe it would happen in a year or two, but it didn't. When Mattie tried to talk to Elaine, Elaine would launch into all these confusing questions: Why shouldn't a woman have the same opportunities as a man? Why couldn't career goals be as important as kitchen goals to a woman? The questions confused Mattie in her head but not in her heart, and Elaine would go off with this see-I-told-you-so attitude when she hadn't really told anything. She'd just asked two or three kind of odd questions.

Robert was reading the paper—sitting on the couch where his father used to sit.

Mattie sliced two tomatoes, put ice in two glasses. Every once in a while she needed to remind them both of what they needed to be about in life: having a family. A Christian family. If they didn't hurry it would be too late to have children. It was her duty to remind. That was a main reason mothers existed. To remind.

And now chances looked slim. She could not understand.

And Robert. Now he was dating that nice woman who didn't dress right: Shirley. He was forty-three for goodness sakes. Shirley was thirty-four, and for some reason Robert had gotten mad when Mattie asked him how old she was. He was like that sometimes.

Mattie did not want to die without grandchildren. She often thought of the links that extended back to Adam, a direct line, like a little dirt road that extended back through forests of time, through a little town that was her mother and father, on back through her grandparents, a little road that went back and back and back across lands and woods and back across to England and back to deserts and the flood and Noah and on back to Adam and Eve. A chain, thousands and thousands of years long, starting way back with Adam and Eve, heading this way, reaching the last link with Robert and Elaine Rigsbee, her own two children, two thousand years after Jesus. And there to be stopped dead forever.

"Come on. It's about ready," said Mattie.

Robert walked to the dinner table. "Where'd the chair bottoms go?" he said.

"They just got up the other morning and walked out the door."

"Ah." Robert smiled. His mother always did have a sense of humor. She had a lot of things, a lot of ways that would have served her well out in the real world if she'd ever gotten out there. But now the world out there was so complicated, she wouldn't last a minute; here she was slowing down now and he didn't want to think about it—except for the fact that Elaine was the one who ought to take care of her if she ever needed it—if Elaine weren't too wrapped up in all her own stuff, Get Out the Vote, and all that crap.

"I got some of the best turnip salet," said Mattie, setting a butter dish on the table. "Patsy Mae come got me
the other morning and she's got five patches of it on her
place and more vines of butterbeans than you can imagine." Mattie sat down at the table, reached for the butter. "Listen, I need to talk to you about how to set up
my will."

"Probably the best thing to do is talk to a lawyer."

"Well, I want to talk to you first. You're the man in the
family."

"Well, the main thing I got to say is see a lawyer. Di-
vide the money down the middle and give Elaine all the
furniture she wants and I'll take the rest. Something
like that. I do want those three lamps. You know that."

"Well, I need to get it all straight." Mattie got up for
the pickle dish, sat back down. "How's Shirley?"

"I don't know."

"You haven't seen her lately?"

"We stopped dating."

"You did? Well, I'm sorry."

Robert took a sip of tea. "You sure?"

"Sure what?"

"Sure you're sorry."

"Well, yes. She was a nice girl and I thought y'all liked
each other."

"I didn't think you liked her that much."

"I liked her okay."

"That's just it. You liked her 'okay.'"

"Let's say the blessing. Do you want to say it?"

"Not especially."

"Dear Lord, bless this food to the nourishment of our

bodies. We pray in Thy precious name. Amen. Well, let's see . . ."

"You talked about the way she dressed."

"Well, there were times when she just didn't fix herself up."

"You made that clear. Pass those potatoes, please."

"Robert, I liked Shirley fine. You don't have to pay so much attention to every little thing I say."

"I know I don't. You don't have to say them either."

"Well, I should be able to speak my mind to my own son. You have to make up your own mind about who you want to marry."

"Cornbread . . . Thanks."

"Don't you want some of this turnip salet?"

"No, thank you."

"You sure?"

"Yes."

After lunch Robert settled again on the couch.

Mattie washed dishes. "Have you got time to clean out my gutters?" she asked. Cleaning out the gutters was one of the things she couldn't do around there anymore. She didn't want to have one of her dizzy spells on the way up a ladder or squatting on the roof, perched over a gutter.

"Yeah, I can clean out the gutters." Robert didn't consider himself a handyman, one of the main reasons he didn't have a house. He'd learned a few things about himself and didn't mind telling people. One thing he didn't like was yard work. That's why he bought himself a condo. Got one while the getting was good, too. He could sell it right now for twice as much as he paid

for it. When someone asked him how he was invest-
ing his money, he said real estate. He didn't say lamps
unless he knew the person asking was interested in
antiques. He had his thirty-two best lamps in his two
bedrooms and the other fifty-six were stored. When they
became worth thousands and thousands he'd start ad-
vertising them one at a time in *Antiques Magazine*.
Many of them had more than doubled in value since he'd
bought them.

"We'll need Finner's aluminum ladder. But I don't believe they're home and I'll bet their garage is locked,"
said Mattie. "Walk out there and see if they're home. If
they're not, the garage might be unlocked, but I doubt it.
Let me finish up here and I'll meet you in the backyard."

Robert walked out to Alora and Finner's. They weren't
home and the garage was locked. Back in the backyard
he said to Mattie, "We got that old heavy ladder stuck up
on the back of the garage, don't we?"

"I believe we do. I'd forgot about it."

Robert got the ladder. It was a long, heavy wooden ladder with round wooden rungs. He leaned it against the
gutter at the back of the house. "Where are some gloves?"
he asked Mattie.

"Right here inside the door. And I got a stick and the
basket over there for you. You can sort of push up the
pine straw out of the gutters."

"I know how to do it."

"I declare I wish Finner and Alora would cut some of
those pine trees down."

"Have you asked them?"

"No."

"Why don't you ask them?"

"They talk about how much they like them all the time. Wind blowing through them and everything."

"Well, I'd ask them if I were you."

Robert put on the gloves. Mattie handed him the stick and basket and he started up the ladder slowly, unsurely.

The top half of the ladder was mostly rotten.

When his hands were four rungs from the top—about a foot below the gutter—he stepped up. His foot crashed through the rung and his leg and knee hit against and popped out the next two higher rungs. His other leg jerked upward frantically, knocking out another rung. One side of the ladder snapped dully, but held together, throwing Robert slightly sideways so that he fell completely through—popping out more rungs. He hung from his armpits and chin on the fourth from the top rung. There were no rungs left between that one and the ones below his feet. He was barely out of reach of the gutter. Reaching the gutter would not have helped; it would only have given him a different place to hang from. He did not have the strength to pull himself up. He was too high to let go, and any maneuvering with his legs could cause the rotten, cracked side of the ladder to break completely through.

"Christamighty," he grunted.

"Robert, I've told you about saying that."

Robert could feel that the ladder was barely holding together. He could feel it but not see it—as if he were standing in the dark on a creaking, swaying platform out over the Grand Canyon.

"Can't you climb up?" asked Mattie.

"I can't do . . . I can't do anything. Not a thing. It's just barely holding together I think. Idn't it?"

"I think it's about to break in two here on the side. What in the world? Let me go get some couch cushions."

"Hurry up. Can you bring a mattress?"

Mattie hurried in the back door, rushed back out with two green couch cushions, and stood directly beneath Robert. She carefully placed one cushion on top of the other on the ground. "Don't fall while I'm under here." She moved the cushions slightly to get the placement right. "I need a plumb line from your foot," she said.

"That's not funny, Mama."

Lamar was speeding down Camp Road with Mattie's rocking chair in the bed of his pickup. He'd wanted to make it for lunch. He'd planned everything to make it for lunch, but then there'd been an emergency call. A woman had sighted a rabid goat in a field and had driven home and called the pound. She knew the goat was rabid because it was foaming at the mouth. The pound called the vet, and then Lamar. Lamar and the vet finally found the woman, who rode with them to the field, but they couldn't find the goat. When they gave up and started to leave the woman screamed, "There he is. There he is. Look at that foam." They all three got out; the woman stood back while Lamar and the vet approached the goat. A gob of white fishing line was hung in the goat's teeth. Lamar pulled up a handful of grass, and the goat came over to eat it. While Lamar straddled the goat's shoulders and held him, the vet extracted the fishing line. But it took awhile.

Lamar turned his pickup into Mattie's driveway, stopped in back, and saw Robert hanging very still from what was left of the ladder, his legs straight, side by side. On the ground directly below him was a single-bed box spring, a mattress, and two green couch cushions on top.

Lamar got out of the truck and walked over. "Why don't he drop?" he asked Mattie who had just come out the door with two big white pillows, one under each arm. She placed them atop the cushions.

"He can now," she said.

"I don't want to drop," said Robert, not moving.

"I could drive my truck under him if it wadn't for those flowers," said Lamar.

"If we had Finner's ladder we could prop that under him," said Mattie.

"Where is it?" asked Lamar.

"In the garage out there, but they've gone somewhere. The garage is locked."

"I can go through that window in back or pop a pane and unlock it if it's locked, slide the ladder out, and then caulk the pane back in later."

"Hurry up. *Do* it," said Robert. "I can't hang here much longer."

"You think it's okay?" Lamar asked Mattie.

"As long as you fix the pane back."

Finner and Alora, returning from visiting Finner's sister-in-law who had had a gall bladder operation, turned in their driveway. Finner had just said they needed a rock at the corner of the driveway and the street so they wouldn't keep wearing away the lawn, when they both saw a pair of blue-jeaned legs—toes pointing up—pulling through the side window into their garage. "Damn! Damn if somebody ain't breaking in the damn garage," said Finner. "You get down on the floor-board. Let me lock the doors. Wait a minute. You wait until I get out, then you lock this door, then get down in the floorboard."

Alora's eyes were as big as plates.

"No," said Finner, "come on in with me and—why the hell is he breaking in the garage instead of the house?"

"Maybe we should just get his licen' number, drive away, and call the sheriff."

"Why in the hell didn't I keep that gun in the glove compartment? Put it under the pillow and sure as hell you need it in the glove compartment. Put it in the glove compartment and—okay, I'm going to . . . if there was some way I could stop up that window then he'd be locked in there."

"We got to do something quick or he'll be gone."

The aluminum extension ladder started out the window.

"Look at that," said Finner. "I'm going in and get the gun and shoot the son of a bitch or hold him inside 'til the law comes. You better go with me—call the police. Let's go. Come on."

They got out of the car and headed for the front door. Finner moved swiftly across the lawn in a combat crouch. Alora was behind him, crouched slightly less, trying to keep up with him. Finner had the front-door key pointed at the front door. But he was shaking so badly he couldn't get it in the key-hole. Then it went in. He moved through

the living room—pointed his finger at the telephone—
and on into the bedroom where he got his pistol out from
under his pillow. He returned through the living room
and into the kitchen. "Don't look it up, Alora, just call
the operator." He looked through the back window and
saw the ladder on the ground, a man's leg extending
through the garage window, another coming out beside
it. Finner went into a crouch, gun in both hands out in
front of his face, arms straight. Beyond the burglar, he
suddenly saw Mattie, and a man hanging from a ladder.
"Call Mattie and tell her to get inside before she gets . . .
wait a minute . . . he . . . I think . . ." It all fell together.
Mattie needed a ladder out there. Somebody was helping
her get a ladder.

"What *is* it?" asked Alora. "What's the matter? I got
the sheriff."

"They needed a ladder out there at Mattie's. Tell them
to never mind."

"Never mind," Alora said into the phone, hung it up,
and walked into the kitchen. "Who is it? What's the
matter?" she said, looking through the window.

"I don't know, but they need a ladder . . ."

"I believe that's the dogcatcher."

"They need a ladder out there. Somebody's hanging.
Damn. Was hanging. Did you see that?"

"You reckon it hurt him?" said Alora.

"I don't think so. All them cushions and stuff."

"Is that Robert?"

"Believe it is. Yep. I tell you one thing. That other boy
almost got hisself shot. I'd a shot him in a heartbeat."

Mattie stared at Robert who had hit squarely on top of the pillows and rolled gently off to the ground. "You all right?"

Robert sat on the ground. "I'm all right except the muscles through my shoulders—from hanging. *Aak*, there goes a spasm." He got up slowly, walked inside. In three trips, Mattie and Lamar put the pillows, cushions, box spring, and mattress back in the house.

Mattie explained to Lamar what had happened.

"I'll clean out your gutters," said Lamar.

"Well, I would appreciate it. It's something I just can't do no more."

Lamar leaned the extension ladder against the gutter and climbed up, holding the stick and basket in one hand.

Alora and Finner walked over into Mattie's yard. As Mattie walked out to meet them, Finner said, "That like to have been one dead dogcatcher."

"What you mean?"

Finner explained. ". . . and I said, 'Call the sheriff, Alora,' and I woulda shot him sure if I hadn't seen you all out here with Robert hanging from the ladder. Why didn't he check out that old ladder before going up it?"

"I hadn't thought about it being rotten," said Mattie.

As she followed Alora and Finner in through the door she heard Elaine's MG and then saw its nose stop behind Lamar's truck which was behind Robert's Ford. "Y'all go on in; I'll be right in." She turned and met Elaine in the yard.

Elaine, a small woman with wire-rimmed glasses, wore a serious expression. She didn't like Finner and

Alora. "Is that our chair?" she asked, looking at the rocker in the back of Lamar's pickup.

"Yes. I almost forgot about it. Robert just fell off a ladder. Or through it. That one on the ground, all broke up."

"Fell off a ladder?" Elaine looked at the ladder. "What in the world?"

"It fell through. He was climbing up to—here, help me get this chair in. The dogcatcher had the chair. He's up on the roof now."

"The dogcatcher? On the roof? Is there a, a dog . . . ?"

"Alora and Finner almost shot him trying to get a ladder out of their garage."

"Shot him?"

"He went in through the garage window. Robert was climbing up to clean out the gutters." Mattie started lifting the chair out of the truck bed.

"Did he get hurt? Here, let me help you. You shouldn't lift that by yourself."

"No, he fell on the mattress and some cushions and pillows."

"How did you get them under him? How did you know he was going to fall?"

Mattie was walking backward, holding on to the front of the chair. "Let's turn sideways so we can both walk straight. He hung from a rung for a right good while. He was going to clean out the gutters. The dogcatcher's doing it now."

Elaine looked up at Lamar. She'd just been reading about how people used to build each other's barns. Maybe that was the good thing about this community. The one good thing.

"That's Lamar, the dogcatcher," said Mattie.

Lamar gave a little salute from the roof, above the back door, where he squatted, one hand in the gutter holding pine straw, wondering if he'd get some apple pie or something like that before he left. That woman down there looked *mad* at him. What the hell had he done to her?

Elaine and Mattie went in the back door. "Well, hey Elaine," said Alora, with a small forced smile.

"Hi, Alora. How are you all getting along? Robert, you hurt?"

"I'm okay. I guess. I just had to hang on to a broken ladder out there for a half hour or so."

"Won't over ten, fifteen minutes," said Mattie. "Get up and move around if you don't want the soreness to settle in."

"That dogcatcher like to been dead," said Finner. "If I hadn't seen y'all out here I would have shot his ass off. Excuse the French, ladies."

"Disgusting," said Elaine under her breath as she sat down on the couch at the other end from Robert. Robert was sitting in his father's place.

"Speak up," said Robert.

Elaine didn't look at Robert. They'd had a bad session on the phone a few nights earlier when Robert called Elaine, having himself been called by Alora who told about Mattie spending all that time hung in the rocker and wondering what could be done now that Mattie was slowing down, that her, Alora's, daughter and son-in-law might be willing to come live with Mattie if Robert thought that would be a good idea, though she, Alora, did not want to be one to pry. It was just that when a seventy-eight-year-old woman sat for six or eight hours in a broken chair then somebody in the family ought to think about doing something in the line of getting assistance, that it would be a drastic step to put Mattie in a rest home, of all places—somebody as mentally fit as she was. Robert had then called Elaine, who said Alora should tend to her own business. Robert had defended Alora and told Elaine she should spend more time with their mother because they were both women.

"Let me fix everybody some coffee," said Mattie. She mentally checked off what she had to offer to eat: pie, ice cream, pound cake, fudge, peanuts. "Who wants iced tea? Or a Coke."

"I'll take a Coke," said Robert.

Robert, thought Mattie. Ladies first. I taught you better than that. "Ladies?"

"I'd like coffee," said Alora.

"Okay, I'll heat some water."

"No, don't go to any trouble, Mattie."

"It's not any trouble."

"Tea, unsweetened if you've got it," said Elaine.

You know what kind of tea I make, thought Mattie. "I think I've got some instant up here I can make," she said. "Robert, you say you want Coke?"

"That's right."

"Finner?"

"Coke's fine. So you got hung up on the ladder?" he said to Robert.

"Sure did."

"That old wooden ladder from out behind the garage?"

"That's the one."

"You didn't check it out to see if it was rotten?"

"Nope, didn't think to."

"Mother, you need some help?" said Elaine, standing, starting to the kitchen.

"No, I'll get it; you keep your seat."

Elaine came into the kitchen anyway.

"I got it," said Mattie. "You go back and sit down. Talk a little." Talk a little to the people you grew up beside but don't hardly ever speak to now that you got a degree, thought Mattie.

"I guess you heard about your mama falling through the chair," Finner said to Robert, in the den.

"Yeah, I did."

"How'd you know about that?" Mattie asked from the kitchen.

"Alora just told me," Robert lied. "Just a minute ago."

"Well, it was right funny in a way," said Mattie. "I wadn't planning on telling anybody, but it got out."

"The rocking chair?" said Elaine, pretending not to know.

"Yes, the rocking chair—the one we just brought in. The dogcatcher fixed it. He's the one got me out. He come after the dog."

"The dog?"

"Oh, that's right, you didn't know about the dog."

"How long were you in the chair?" asked Robert.

"A few hours." Nobody had to know about "All My Children."

No one spoke.

"Well, Robert, how's your work going?" Alora asked. She was sitting across from him.

"What kind of dog?" Elaine asked her mother in the kitchen.

"Fine," said Robert. "Been a little slow lately."

"A little fice," said Mattie.

"You didn't call the SPCA?"

Mattie thought about Wesley. "Where they keep the juvenile delinquents?"

"No, that's the YMRC. The SPCA is the Society for Prevention of Cruelty to Animals."

"I wadn't being cruel to him. I just needed the dog-catcher. I can't keep up this place and a dog, too. You know that. I'm surprised I kept him as long as I did."

"Mother, they would have tried to save the dog's life."

"Here, take this Coke over to Robert and Finner and pour some peanuts out of that jar into this bowl."

"Did you hear what I said, Mother? The dog will be put to sleep now if nobody picks him up within thirty days."

"Why don't you go get him, take him home. You could use a dog. Here, the coffee's ready. Get those peanuts over there, would you? Pour them in here." The whole family hadn't been together with neighbors since Paul died, thought Mattie, and Elaine wants to talk about a dog. Mattie carried a cup of coffee to Alora.

Alora was talking to Robert about the dogcatcher. "Well, Finner would've shot him sure as the world. We keep a loaded pistol under Finner's pillow. You figure it'll be night if you ever need one. And I take it with me when I go on my walk if Fred's not at home down there at the end of the road. I ain't going to have nobody jump out of them woods and get me. Wrap a Kleenex around it so nobody'll notice. Little . . . what is it Finner, a .22?"

"Yep, .22."

My God, thought Elaine. Why would anybody jump on you?

"Okay now," said Mattie, returning to the kitchen, "who wants cake, who wants apple pie, who wants ice cream, or a little ice cream along with one of the others?"

"I pass," said Elaine.

"Pass!" said Alora. "Good gracious, girl."

"Cake and ice cream," said Finner. "Your mama makes the best pound cake I ever eat," Finner said to Robert.

Alora, with her coffee cup to her lip, eyed Finner.

"Alora, what do you want?" asked Mattie.

"Well, I don't need anything, Lord knows," said Alora, "but I'll take a little pie . . . with a tiny scoop of ice cream."

"You want pie and ice cream, don't you, Robert?" said Mattie.

"Yes ma'am."

Alora looked at Robert and Elaine. "Well, well," she said. They were all sitting in the den except Mattie who was fixing the dessert in the kitchen. "This is the first time I known y'all to be here together since I don't know when. Since Paul died I guess."

"When did y'all move here anyway?" asked Finner.

"'58," said Robert.

Elaine picked up a *Biblical Recorder* to see what the Baptists were up to. She turned on the lamp beside her. She had wandered spiritually since her sophomore year in college—not going to church at all until she met, at a cocktail party a few years ago, a Unitarian minister with whom she agreed on every topic she could think of. She went to his church in Raleigh at least six or eight times a year.

Mattie came into the den with a tray holding the desserts. "Now the pie ain't hot," she said, "but it's good cold. . . . We don't need that light," she said to Elaine.

"I'm trying to read."

"If you cooked it, it's good," said Finner.

They all heard sounds of Lamar walking across the roof toward the ladder.

"Lord, I forgot the dogcatcher," said Mattie.

"Whose piece of cake is *that*?" asked Elaine.

"It's mine," said Mattie.

"Mother, the doctor told you not to eat *any* sweets."

"I know it. But I hadn't had enough to hurt anything and if he finds sugar when I go back I'll cut them out altogether. But what if I cut them out altogether and went back and didn't have no blood in my sugar then how—"

"Sugar in your blood," said Elaine.

"What'd I say?"

"You said blood in your sugar."

"That's probably what it amounts to," said Robert.

Lamar knocked on the back door.

"Anyway," said Mattie, going toward the door, stopping to finish. "If they don't find no sugar this next time then I'll know that eating a little bit along ain't going to hurt anything, whereas if I'd cut it out altogether, then I wouldn't know whether I could eat just a little bit and still get along okay." She opened the back screen. "Come on in. Y'all, this is Lamar. I forgot your last name."

"Benfield." Lamar looked around—saw apple pie. Hot damn, he thought.

"Don't you want a little dessert?" asked Mattie.

"You might force a little on me," said Lamar. "How y'all doing?"

"You like to been dead a while ago," said Finner.

"You sure did," said Alora.

"Well, I'm glad I'm still alive."

"Did you want pie?" Mattie asked Lamar from the kitchen.

"Yeah."

"How about a little ice cream?"

"I could handle that. You hurt yourself?" Lamar said to Robert.

"No, I don't think so, but I'll be a little sore probably."

"You were sore the other morning, won't you, Mrs. Rigsbee," said Lamar.

"I sure was."

There was a quiet spell. Mattie couldn't think of anything to say from the kitchen. She brought Lamar his food and drink and then went back and got a board for the rocker seat, put it across the seat, and sat down. Robert and Elaine were sitting on the couch and the rest sat in chairs and held their plates, eating dessert.

"You're eating ice cream, too?" said Elaine to Mattie.

"This was all that was left—not enough to sneeze at. It's not hardly a spoonful."

"I don't know about that sugar in the blood either," said Alora. "Dr. Harmon told my mama she had sugar in the blood and I don't know if she did or not. He got her started on insular and she died seven years later when she was sixty-four, which is right young. I wondered a lot of times if she'd lived longer if she hadn't a got started on that stuff. I don't think he ever checked her but once. Right at the beginning."

"Insular?" said Robert.

"Yeah. Insular."

Elaine looked upward.

"I got to go watch the ball game," said Finner, standing. "You coming?" he asked Alora.

"Go ahead, I'll be on."

"You can turn it on here," said Mattie. "Are the Braves playing?"

"Yeah."

"I like the Braves. Turn it on, Robert."

"I declare they got so many niggers playing these days," said Alora. "There was a team on the other day, I forgot who it was, they had a nigger playing every position but third base."

"You don't see many nigger third basemen," said Finner. "Third base is the hot corner."

"Excuse me," said Elaine. She stood, walked down the hall and to the bathroom, closed the door, pulled down her slacks and panties, sat down on the commode, put her elbows on her knees, her palms on her chin. I'll wait them out, she thought. She stared at the little space heater. Her mother used no central heat or air conditioning until the outside temperature was down in the forties or up in the nineties. Elaine often tried to explain to her mother how she was saving very little money if any in the long run.

Ten minutes later when Elaine heard the back screen

close, she stood, pulled up her panties and slacks, flushed the commode and went back to the den. The ball game was playing loudly.

"Well, I've got to be going," said Elaine. "I'm supposed to be at a meeting in Chapel Hill at four."

"Nice to have met you," said Lamar, holding a piece of fudge in his mouth.

Elaine walked over to Mattie in the kitchen. "I'll see you soon, Mama. Take care of yourself, don't eat so many sweets, and don't fall through another chair."

"I don't know what my weight'll do without my sweets," said Mattie. "I've fell off I don't know how much."

"Well, you do what the doctor says. He knows better than you."

Robert stood. "I got to get going, too."

"Thanks for cleaning out my gutters," said Mattie, and laughed.

"You're welcome. I'd like to know why we kept that ladder around here."

Mattie stood on the back steps as Robert and Elaine walked across the back lawn to their cars. "Come back when you can stay awhile," she said.

"How you like your MG?" Robert asked Elaine when they reached her car.

"I like it okay. It's fun to drive." Elaine watched Mattie go back inside. "She doesn't look good to me, Robert."

"Seemed all right to me."

"She just didn't look good. She *has* fallen off some."

"You stop eating a pound of candy a day and you'd fall off too."

"It's not funny."

"Well, she seemed all right to me. I got to get going; good to see you," said Robert. "She'll be all right."

"Good to see you, Robert." Elaine got into her car, cranked up, backed out of the drive, and drove away.

Robert stood in the backyard. He looked at the aluminum ladder. Somebody needed to carry it back to Finner's garage out there, and clean up what was left of the old wooden one. He walked over, grabbed the aluminum ladder, lifted it. It was surprisingly light.

He held it horizontally in one hand as he walked out to Finner's garage. The garage door was open now. He went inside and hung the ladder in its place along the wall. It was cool and damp in the garage. His shoulders felt very weak from hanging so long. Thank goodness his mother had put the mattress and cushions and pillows under him. "Need a plumb line from your foot." She could always come up with something funny in tense times. He couldn't. Not like she could.

There was a table of jars there in the back of the garage. The floor was hard packed dirt. It was so cool. Yeah, he hadn't inherited that sense of humor of hers. He'd try little jokes at the cash register at the CFM— with customers—and it never worked. They'd look at him like he was crazy. He couldn't cook like her, or tend to things. If he could tend to the Convenient Food Mart the way she'd tended to him when he was growing up, then he'd be moving on up the ladder of success. He guessed he was a little more like his daddy than he was like her.

"What you want?" said Finner, standing behind him.

Robert jumped; a spasm caught him. "Yeow." He arched back his shoulders, thrusting out his chest.

"What's the matter?"

"Just a catch," he grunted.

"That like to been one dead dogcatcher. He better fix back that windowpane, too."

"I think he said he was," grunted Robert, bending over crossing his arms.

"Good thing Mattie put all them cushions down."

"It sure is. You know what she said when she was putting them under there?" Robert stood back up straight.

"What?"

"Said she needed a plumb line from my foot so she'd know where to put them."

"Is that right? A plumb line."

"It was a joke."

"Oh. Yeah, well, I hope I can get around like she does when I'm however old she is."

"Yeah, me too. Seventy-eight. She's seventy-eight."

In Mattie's backyard, Robert picked up the pieces of the broken ladder. He put the smaller pieces in the garbage can by the garage and leaned the larger pieces beside it. He glanced at the back of the house. It was a wonder his mother hadn't come out. She was watching the ballgame with that dogcatcher. Well, good. He walked to his car, got in, backed down the driveway, and drove away.

"I need to pay you for my chair," Mattie said to Lamar. "I hadn't even had a chance to look at it good. Let me see it." She examined the chair.

"Won't nothing to it. Just glue and a brace. I had everything in my shop. I got a little shop behind my house. It'll be, oh, a couple of dollars."

"Just two dollars. You sure? Things are mighty high these days."

"That'll cover it."

Mattie got her billfold from her purse, pulled out two dollars and handed them to Lamar. "How about for cleaning out my gutters?"

"Well, that's, ah, that's *on the house*. Ha!"

Mattie puzzled, looked at him. "Well, that's mighty nice, but you don't have to . . . Oh, *on the house*. I get it." She laughed. "Like the gutters. On the house. Well, I appreciate your kindness."

"That dinner yesterday was worth a hundred dollars."

"Well, it won't *that* much. Anyway, you could charge the regular fee and buy a little something for your nephew out at the RC. It must be pretty awful him being out there at that place."

"Yeah, I guess it is."

"Well, thanks for everything you've done."

"Let me know when there's something else."

"The only other thing I can think of is I need a new top for my well house. That thing is so old, and it leaks. So if you're looking for something to do, for some work, I'd pay you."

"Okay, maybe I can fix you up. I'll let you know. Maybe I can pick it up one afternoon, fix it at home."

Lamar and Mattie walked out into the backyard. Mattie thought about that Wesley boy and how she used to visit Paul's cousin's husband in jail. Jesus said to do that. It was clear, in the Scriptures. And that kind of visiting made sense for some balance in the world, some balance against all those people with so much money who all the time buy buy buy. Greed greed greed. Never doing anything for anybody. "You think you'll be visiting your nephew?" she said. "Wesley?"

"Wesley. Yeah, I'll probably go see him sometime," said Lamar. "Take him some cigarettes."

"Well, when you go see him, stop by and I'll send him a little something to eat." That scripture, Jesus talking about visiting prisoners and all, was "Inasmuch as ye have done it unto one of the least of these my brethren ye have done it unto me."

Lamar drove away and Mattie went back in the house. She walked over to the rocker and pushed it to be sure it rocked evenly. She studied the brace and the way it had been put in. Right nice work. What was that? . . . Stove eye. Red hot! From making the coffee. She hurried over and turned it off. She was going to burn the house down if she wasn't careful. I declare, she thought. I'm slowing down, that's all there is to it. I could be like Aunt Alba; she just all of a sudden started slowing down *fast.* Or a stroke, like Turnie. That could happen to me. It could happen any time. But I think I got a few good years left. Of course there's Mrs. Bledsoe who slowed down real slow and nobody thought she would ever wear out and Frances came to live with her which is something I don't know about. I don't think I'd want Robert or Elaine here. They wouldn't be happy. They need a chance to have families of their own. Besides, I don't think I want to live with anybody. I've lived with somebody all my life and took care and took care and took care and I've done a good job of it: clothed and fed and cared for a husband and two children for all my life and now I'm enjoying sitting at night and reading my Bible and I don't want somebody moving in. But look at Mary Belle there in a rest home, and Phoebe Sue and Dorcus and they just sit there and I can see Phoebe Sue and Dorcus as clear as if it was yesterday riding in that mule race, their faces red and them laughing up a storm, bouncing up and down on them mules and now there they sit every day that goes by, there they sit. Of course some of those places are right nice I suppose.

Mattie went into the living room and sat at the piano and played "What a Friend We Have in Jesus." She looked at the pictures on the piano.

Well, after all was said and done, after all was said and done, she had Jesus. She would always have Jesus. But. But it wadn't his way to come in and keep you company. You couldn't cook for him.

IV

On Sunday morning Mattie woke early and couldn't go back to sleep. She was thinking of that boy. Wesley. She pictured him sitting at a picnic table in the prison yard looking through that tall fence with the barbed wire along the top. She saw Lamar—with his hat on— walking up to Wesley and placing a paper sack with a piece of her apple pie in it on the table in front of him. He'd open it and look at it and maybe not even be interested. What an awful way to live even if you are young. But he might deserve prison: stealing a car, taking something that didn't belong to him. She bet the food he got wasn't very good.

It was still dark outside, but she couldn't sleep. She stretched to see how sore she was. The soreness from falling through the chair was almost gone. It had been almost a week. Of course they would all know about it in Sunday school this morning. They would all be asking her about it and she'd have to tell them all. Then there would be those in other classes who'd need to hear before church, and then those who still hadn't heard first-hand would need to hear after church. She'd tell them all she was slowing down and didn't quite have the memory she used to have. She could say all that without complaining really. She didn't intend to start complaining. Not like Sarah Mae and that new woman who talked about her fingers. Mattie had more finger problems than that woman ever did. Mattie's thumb and index finger on her right hand wouldn't come together with any strength at all. But she didn't complain, except to Robert and Elaine, occasionally. She reserved the right to complain to her own family.

She stretched again. She would fix a slow breakfast, scramble her eggs for a change and fix some grits. Maybe she should start eating grits every morning—to keep from falling off so fast.

She threw back the covers, stood; yes, the soreness was about gone—because she'd kept moving. She wasn't about to give over to a little fall through a chair.

She put on her housecoat and sweater and went to the bathroom. Thank goodness she'd always been regular. No problems there. Because she ate so well. Anybody who ate all the vegetables she did couldn't help but be regular—didn't need Milk of Magnesia like Alora did. And never the first hint of a hemorrhoid.

She walked into the kitchen, turned on the light and saw through the window that the eastern sky was dark red. It was her favorite time of the day. She stepped out onto the back step. It was cool. She also liked it when it was cold and she could stand there taking in the cold morning while the sky was red, and time stopped, stood still, and rested for a minute. People thought that time never stood still, except in Joshua when the sun stood still; but she knew that for a minute before sunrise when the sky began to lighten, showing dark, early clouds, there was often a pause when nothing moved, not even time, and she was always happy to be up and in that moment; sometimes she tried to stand perfectly still, to not move with time not moving, and it seemed that if she were not careful she might slip out of this world and into another. That made the moment risky, bright shining, and very still at the same time. She hoped that when her time came, it would be close to morning, and she could wait for the still moment.

Mattie's Sunday school departmental assembly—one of the three adult groups—was held in a large meeting room on the second floor in the back of the church. Small classrooms fed into the large room. After the twenty-minute assembly the group always split into same-sex and -age groups and went into the small meeting rooms where they held classes for about thirty minutes.

The department president, Martha Bowers, standing behind a podium, called the assembly to order and opened with a prayer. Officers had been elected two Sundays ago, and Mattie was now vice-president. Of course, a vice-president never had to do much, unless the president was sick, but Mattie liked the sound of "vice-president."

Mattie sat in her usual place on the second row. After the prayer they all stood and sang "The Church's One Foundation." Then Martha announced that Clarence Vernon, the head deacon, would be around any minute with an announcement about the Lottie Moon offering. Lottie Moon was a missionary who had worked long ago in China, and in whose name money was collected for foreign missions each year. For the past five years, Mattie had been in charge. She was sure that this morning Clarence would announce that she would again be in charge. Her job would be to call up the president of each Sunday school assembly in the church and tell them where to pick up the envelopes. Then she would coordinate the whole affair, collecting money and making reports to the church treasurer. She would visit each assembly on Sunday mornings and make announcements and reports. Then at Christmas the money would be donated to missions.

When Clarence came in, he sat beside Mattie while waiting to make his announcement. He leaned over and whispered, "Mattie, you do want to do the Lottie Moon again this year, don't you?"

Mattie looked at him, smiled, nodded yes.

"You do such a good job."

"I enjoy it."

Clarence stood and made several short announcements, the last one being that Mattie Rigsbee would be heading up the Lottie Moon again.

Martha then gave the lesson, another hymn was sung, a prayer said, and the meeting broke up so people could go to their small classes. Mattie said a word or two to several people on the way to her class. When she arrived, three of the regulars were already there: Martha, Beatrice, and Carrie, the class president. The others usually lingered in the assembly room a little while.

As soon as Mattie cleared the doorway, before she even had a chance to sit down, Beatrice said, "Well, Mattie, I hear you got stuck in your rocking chair." Mattie had known Beatrice would be the first one to mention it. Beatrice was the secretary-treasurer of the class, and knew everything about everybody and was prepared at the drop of a hat to *say* anything about anybody. Her specialties were sickness, soreness, death, separations, miscarriages, and car wrecks.

Mattie didn't like Beatrice. "That's right. I left the bottom out. My memory's getting so I can't remember a thing."

"Lord, have mercy, I can't remember nothing no more either," said Beatrice.

"I can't either," said Martha, smoothing her dress under her legs, the wicker in her chair bottom popping. Martha was direct. She got to any point immediately with a straight look, straight mouth, straight head. Mattie liked her, felt secure with her, enjoyed speaking her mind to her. "Can't remember nothing no more," said Martha, staring without a smile at Mattie, and ready to talk.

"Somebody was telling me something about getting

old and buying bananas," said Beatrice. "Something about green bananas."

"Johnny Arnold," said Martha, "told about how he was getting so old he was afraid to buy green bananas." She smiled.

"That was it!" said Beatrice and laughed.

Carrie and Mattie smiled.

"Don't you get it?" Beatrice asked Mattie.

She didn't get it but she wouldn't admit it. "Yes, I got it."

"You might die before they get ripe," said Martha.

"Right," said Mattie. "Well, that's like Old Mrs. Bledsoe. You heard about that. She said—"

Beatrice interrupted—"if she'd known she was going to live until she was ninety-four she would have bought a new bed."

She interrupted, thought Mattie, and on top of that she got it wrong. "What she said was," said Mattie, "'If I'd known I was going to live this long I'd of bought a new mattress.' That's what she said. I was there when she said it."

Beatrice looked stunned, then recovered.

"Let's get started," said Carrie. The others had come in. "Beatrice, would you lead us in a word of prayer?"

There, I went and did it, thought Mattie. Lord, forgive me. I shouldn't get mad at her like that. Dear Lord, please help me to control my anger and to love and tolerate Beatrice, a Christian. At least she says she is.

Mattie thought about Lamar and Wesley. She wondered if they were saved. Surely Wesley wasn't. Maybe Lamar, but she doubted it: the way he kept his hat on in the house indicated something, a lack of something. But maybe he'd been saved when he was a little boy, the way Robert had been saved when he was only nine. And Robert once sang the most beautiful little solos with the Primary Choir and then in the Junior Choir; but then he lost complete interest in singing. Seemed like he was embarrassed, and that was the last thing in the world she had wanted to happen. A man embarrassed to sing is a man incomplete somehow. Paul would never sing either. She never heard Paul sing a single word for as long as she knew him—over fifty years. And she'd heard him say only one prayer, and that was a blessing, at a family reunion when Steven Purvis had been asked by somebody who didn't know what they were doing to say the blessing and Steven, panic in his face and eyes, had turned to look at Paul standing beside him and without leaning over to Paul or moving his head said, "I can't pray!" and Paul had closed his eyes and said "Dear God, bless this food to the nourishment of our bodies, Amen." Mattie had felt almost stricken. It was so unlike Paul to say a prayer out loud. Surely he'd prayed silently; he was a Christian. But she'd never known when, or what for.

Beatrice was still praying. God forgive me, thought Mattie. If I get mad at my Christian friends what would I do with non-Christians. I'm supposed to love them too, even the communists. There might be some communists, thought Mattie, that I'd like more than Beatrice. At least if they talked I wouldn't know what they were saying. But if it was some Russian man my age who had a shop and made things, maybe sharpened saws and made little things out in the shop, had big hands, wore rough clothes and would come in and sit down beside me on the piano bench and sing a hymn with me, I know I'd like that man better than I like Beatrice whether he could speak English or not.

"Let's open our quarterlies, page forty-three," said Carrie, standing behind a podium in the small room. The others sat in their wicker-bottomed chairs. Two windows were along one wall. A bulletin board and a chalk board were along other walls. "Mattie would you read the scripture?"

Mattie found and read the scripture printed in the quarterly at the beginning of the lesson. It was from Jeremiah 31, about the new covenant that God was to make with the house of Israel, and included "And they shall teach no more every man his neighbour, and every man his brother saying, Know the Lord: for they shall all know me, from the least of them unto the greatest of them, saith the Lord: for I will forgive their iniquity, and I will remember their sin no more." Mattie had thought about that Wesley boy when she studied it last night, and had wondered where that other scripture about "the least of these" was—doing unto the least being the same as doing for Jesus.

She would have to look into some way of doing something for Wesley. There was so much promise in his kin, his uncle, Lamar. He had a good heart. She could tell. He had a straightforwardness to him. He didn't shirk around in the shadows like so many young people nowadays. He'd *speak* to a person. So many young people at church wouldn't speak. Their parents didn't make them—didn't seem to care whether they spoke to old people or not. She'd elbow them, and make them speak, by golly.

When Lamar stopped wearing that hat inside, decided to polish his shoes and get some crease in his pants he could be downright pleasant to be around.

When the class was over and the closing prayer finished, Carrie said, "Mattie, I want to hear about you falling through your rocking chair."

"Good gracious," said Mattie. "It won't nothing. I just fell through." She decided to show them the bruises on the backs of her legs. "Close that door," she said. Beatrice closed the door. "Look a-here," she said. She raised her dress and turned around so they could all see.

"Lord have mercy, Mattie."

"Good gracious in the morning."

"I'll swanee, Mattie."

Mattie liked that about herself: how she'd go ahead and do little things the others wouldn't do—like raise her dress to show off a bruise, and she could sense that people liked that about her, counted on her for it. "Yes," she said, "it was just awful, and funny in a way."

Mattie walked alone to the church sanctuary, shouldered against several young people to get them to speak to her. She knew that courteousness had started on the way out with television and integration and a man on the moon. She wished somebody would put their finger exactly on the connections so something could be done about it. And she knew the weather had been affected by those people landing on the moon. No question about it. It was all mixed in with reasons for the great decline of courtesy. In some ways she was glad it was now that she was slowing down and not forty years from now, having had to live through the decline of *everything* good.

She walked into the sanctuary, down the aisle, toward her seat, left side, halfway. Carrie would be along in a minute to sit with her. She moved into the middle and sat down. Some people would sit on the end of an empty pew and then everybody had to crawl over them. And those young people in the back were so noisy these days. Three Sundays ago, before the service started, she had gotten up, walked back there, and told them if they couldn't be quieter to go outside. They got quiet, too. If the Lord's house got to be not sacred then there could be no place that was sacred, no place on earth for the rest of the earth to compare itself to.

The sanctuary began to fill up. Buck Bosser and Phil Gates walked in along the empty pew behind her, bent over and asked her about getting stuck in the rocking chair. She laughed quietly, turned to look up at them. They moved on. Why did she even think about keeping it a secret anyway? It was fun. Phil had said he wanted to hear all about it after the service. He would be standing in his place outside after the service. He and Buck and Buck's wife, what's her name, there by the pole supporting the rain shelter leading to the education building. Mae and George would be over by the other pole. She would tell them all, and have a good time doing it.

The choir members filed in, one by one in their robes. She'd stopped singing in the choir when she realized for sure that she was slowing down. She'd sung there for over thirty years and had listened to some folks stay far beyond their prime. Mrs. Brown, bless her heart, had stayed until she squeaked and went flat. And she, Mattie, had begun to feel the pressure of the performances; it got so it took her longer to learn her part. She had sense enough to step down. Nobody begged her to stay either, but that was all right.

And there singing alto on the front row, Marie Lloyd with all that makeup. If Marie only knew how much better she looked without it. Mattie was almost glad she couldn't see that far anymore. She would never forget the Christmas Marie was sick and the choir went Christmas caroling and went out of their way to go by Marie's house. Marie was inside in the living room, on the couch, watching television. Bill told them to come on in; they did, and there Marie was sitting on the couch in her bathrobe *without any makeup*. Mattie marveled over how much better she looked sick, without makeup, than she did well and with makeup. She had such good features.

It was time for the scripture. Mattie read along. It was the time people needed to be most quiet, but some of the young people didn't pay any attention at all to what was going on. Some of the adults didn't. That Denise Singletary was as likely to be coming in as going out with that brat of a little boy she had no idea how to manage. Always sitting down there at the front. That child climbing up, looking back, making faces and noises, Denise sitting there as if he didn't exist and then when it was far too late, bending over and saying something to the child which the child ignored, of course—it won't the child's fault—and then saying something again, and then when the whole church was looking, disturbed and missing whatever was going on, she would walk out holding the little crying screaming thing on her shoulder. The child was cute on those rare occasions he behaved—he had potential.

That afternoon, Wesley Benfield, stringy blond hair down his neck and over his ears, a few tufts of hair here and there on his face, including the beginnings of a blond mustache, sat on a bench at a picnic table looking through red-rimmed eyes across the Young Men's Rehabilitation Center yard at the fence. What a goddamned joke this whole place was. He hooked his one long fingernail—the little one on his right hand—under a splinter on the table, pulled it up. The splinter cracked from the table as it widened, more and more wood coming up. He could make a weapon if it kept coming up. It was pointed. He looked around. He carefully raised the piece of wood. Pop, it broke from the table. Not enough for a weapon. He'd like to take that picnic table apart piece by piece. He'd like to take the whole goddamned institution apart piece by piece.

His eyes moved along the fence. He shook the hair back out of his eyes. Every day he looked for a hole in the fence, a ruptured link, a break, a slight opening of some sort, something nobody else would notice. No luck.

He wanted a cigarette so bad he didn't know what to do.

If he could find a hole, an opening, he'd be out of that place as fast as—he looked around, then spoke to himself: "I'd be out of here as fast as a greasy string through a duck's ass." He scratched the back of his leg.

He noticed Norman, the guard, at the gate, checking in some old woman.

He sucked air in through his teeth, inhaled it, pretending he was smoking. Lamar had said he would bring him a carton of Salems. Wesley smoked Salems because John Prine had a pack of them along with a glass of water sitting on a stool on stage at a concert one time. Wesley had been on the front row watching, and ever since then he'd smoked Salems. Prine was cool. Wesley had tried to sing some of his songs. Learned a few chords on a guitar. Wrote a few songs himself, the words anyway. Good songs. Lamar had said he was going to bring him a John Prine tape with "Spanish Pipedream" and "Please Don't Bury Me" on it, but he hadn't. Where the hell was Lamar anyway? He should have been there already.

The old woman was talking to Norman. Norman was pointing . . . at him, it looked like. Wesley looked over his shoulder and saw Benny and Gerald over by the wall. Norman must be pointing at them. For sure it won't him. He didn't know no goddamned old woman.

Mattie looked at the young man sitting alone at the picnic table. He was wearing a blue shirt—like the others were wearing.

The guard held the gate open and Mattie walked through it and toward the young man. There's nothing to be afraid of, she thought. All these families are out here, scattered around.

She's headed at *me*, thought Wesley. He looked over

his shoulder again. She's got to be coming to one of them guys. I ain't done nothing to her.

He don't look like Jesus, thought Mattie.

I'm getting the hell out of here, thought Wesley. She was headed right at him. Headed right between his eyes, carrying a covered tin pan and a paper sack.

He stood, lifted his foot over his seat and onto the ground, looked around at Benny and Gerald, back at the old woman, who had stopped right there at his table.

"Wesley?" she said.

He froze. Seemed like she was saying that like she had brought something for him—that in the pan. He started his foot back, rested it on the seat. "You got a cigarette?" he said.

"A cigarette?"

"Yeah."

She set the pan on the table. "No I don't have no cigarette. You don't need one either."

"What's in there?"

"A piece of cake, piece of pie."

"Who's it for?"

"You're Wesley, ain't you?"

"Yeah, I'm Wesley." He sat, slowly. What the hell was going on? What kind of goddamn trick was this. Somebody out to poison his ass?

"I brought you a little something. I'm Mattie Rigsbee." He's not a bad-looking boy at all. A little wrung out maybe. "I can tell you smoke by your color."

"Well, good for you." Wesley eyed the paper bag. "I

don't smoke *now*. I ain't got no cigarettes. Ain't had none for two days."

"You stop smoking and your color will improve."

"Who gives a shit whether my color improves."

Mattie stared at him. "I do. And listen, son, you shouldn't ever talk that way around a lady."

Wesley's head fell forward slightly while he stared into Mattie's eyes; he suddenly laughed, looking away, staring far away out over the green trees, covering his mouth with his hand while he laughed, then looked back at Mattie as it hit him. He stopped laughing. "Are you my grandma?"

Bad teeth, thought Mattie. "No, I'm not."

She might be lying, thought Wesley. "My grandma's alive somewhere. One of them, I know." He looked around to see who was looking. This was the craziest thing in the world. Here was this old woman who could very well be his grandma come to see *him. Telling him what to do.* Well shit, this was the funniest thing in the world. "You brought me some cake and pie?"

"I'm going to take it back if you don't apologize."

"Who sent you out here? You sure you ain't my grandma?"

"I know about you because of Lamar, your uncle. Do you want this piece of cake and pie?" Mattie was still standing.

"Yeah. I'll take a piece of cake and pie. I apologize." He looked around.

"I put it on a paper plate in case you didn't want to eat it right now and—"

"I'll eat it right now."

Mattie opened the tin container. She lifted her foot over the bench to sit down, and noticed that she was still a little sore from falling through the chair. She'd tell him about falling through the chair. People liked that story and she'd gotten it down pretty well. Everybody else knew about it; why not him? "I'm a little sore from falling through a chair," she said as she sat down slowly.

"What's in the paper sack?"

"Iced tea and a plastic fork. I brought the tea in a mason jar. I got so many mason jars I don't know what to do."

"The iced tea they got here is rotten. Tastes like it's got rotten oranges in it."

"I've tasted tea like that." She pulled the tea out of the paper sack and set it between them, twisted off the top. "Well, this ain't rotten. There you go. You can start on that." From the tin container she lifted out the paper plate with a piece of cold apple pie and a piece of pound cake on it. Well, he was the one person since Monday who hadn't wanted to know every single detail about her falling through the chair. She pulled out the plastic fork wrapped in a paper towel and laid it on the table. "Help yourself."

Wesley looked at the plate with the big piece of pie, big hunk of cake. The apple pie was not runny. It was solid, the apples held together with a cold solid filling. It was thick, with a faint hint of sparkling sugar on the crust. Resting beside it was the thick hunk of pound cake, visibly moist. And the jar of tea with ice cubes, the jar looking wet and cold. He looked at Mattie's face. She was looking at him. He reached for the jar of tea, sipped, then drank. He put the tea down, picked up the fork and cut a big corner off the cake, stuck it from the top with the fork—it hung together with moisture—and put it in his mouth. It was the best thing he'd ever eaten in his life. "That's the best cake I ever had in my life."

"Well, I'm glad you like it. But, listen, you should be more careful about your language."

Wesley wanted to finish the cake so he could get to the pie. He looked around. It was a wonder somebody wasn't coming over to get some. "Where's Lamar?"

"I don't know. I didn't tell anybody I was coming, I just took off on the spur of the moment after I washed my dinner dishes."

Wesley was eating the pie. It was the best pie he'd ever had. The cinnamon. That was it, and the apples and crust had a little crispy crunch. "You seen Lamar today?"

"No, I saw him yesterday. He fixed a chair of mine."

"In his shop?"

"I reckon so."

"He's got one hell of a shop."

Mattie decided to let the "hells" and "damns" go. They let them go on television. "Well, he did a nice job on the chair."

"He's supposed to come out here today. He called and told them he would."

"How long are you supposed to be in here?"

"I don't know. My lawyer moved to Virginia and I ain't been able to get a new one." He put the last piece of pie in his mouth.

"You stole a car?"

"That's the thing. I didn't steal it. These guys I was with stole it." Wesley swallowed. "We'd been sort of drinking and it was all their idea, all their execution. They executed the whole thing. They—"

"Use your napkin."

Wesley wiped his mouth. "They got in first and everything and the only way I had to get home was to ride. Then the law found out about Holder. Ferren Holder. Ferren was driving. His old man made him go to the police and tell them that it was all mine and Morris's fault, Morris Griffin, and they believed it, man. They *believed* it, and that's the last chance I've had, and when I get out of here I'm going to . . ." That pie was *good*, thought Wesley. ". . . to cut his head off."

"Well, I'm sorry you have to live in here," said Mattie, looking around. "But if you live in society you have to follow the rules."

"Rules? That's a joke."

Wesley finished the tea, sucked on an ice cube, spit it back into the jar, turned the jar up, let the ice cube fall into his mouth and shuffled it as he talked. "If Lamar'd give me a place to live I might could get out of here. You got a extra room?"

"Oh, no, I couldn't . . . I don't have a room. I couldn't do that." Mattie envisioned talking with Elaine, Robert, Pearl, Alora: "This young prisoner is coming to live with me." But there was that doing unto the least of these scripture. What if she said, "Jesus is coming to live with me"?

"If I could get somewhere to live. Lamar said he would help me out, but I don't know if he is or not."

"How old are you?"

"Sixteen."

"Well, son, I hope something works out. I know it must be terrible to live here. But I'm too old to rent rooms. I'm slowing down."

"There he is! *Lamar*."

Lamar was talking to the guard. He waved.

"I'll speak to him on the way out," said Mattie. "I got to get going on back. My sister usually comes by on a Sunday evening. Here he comes. I'll speak to him before I get up."

"Hey, Mrs. Rigsbee," said Lamar, walking up.

"Hey there."

"I stopped by your house to get Wesley a little something to eat, like you said." He handed a small paper sack to Wesley. "Here's your cigarettes."

"Thank God."

"I visit around on Sundays," said Mattie, "so I just figured I'd come on out here and visit and bring a little something myself. I just said to Wesley here that I got to get going. I told him about you fixing my chair."

"I'll fix that well-house roof for you, too. I'll come by one day next week to get it."

"Let me know when you're coming. Give me a call."

Lamar looked at the pan and paper sack. "She brought you something?"

"Best cake and pie I ever eat," said Wesley, blowing smoke.

"Well, thank you," said Mattie, slowly standing. "I got to get going."

Wesley eyed Mattie through the smoke. She might really be my grandma, he thought, coming here to check me out, see if she wants to keep me. She might just found out I even exist and she's got a million dollars stuffed away and I'm going to her house and live in a cabin out back and she's going to buy me a 4 by 4 and any damn thing else I want. "Thank you for bringing all that."

"Well, it won't nothing. You all behave yourselves. Maybe I'll get back out here to see you again." She started off, stopped, turned, and said to Lamar, "I'm still a little sore from that chair."

"Well, I guess so."

"Good-bye."

Lamar picked up the mason jar. "Is this hers?"

"Yeah."

Lamar started after her, handed her the jar. She grabbed his arm and stopped him from turning back around. She whispered, "Do you suppose he'd let me get his teeth fixed."

"Well, yeah, I guess so, if you want to."

"I just wondered. I'll be seeing you."

Lamar sat back down at the picnic table with Wesley. Wesley took a deep drag on the cigarette, blew smoke through his mouth, then nose. "Is she my grandma?" he asked. "My mama's mama?"

"Not that I know of. Why?"

"I just wondered if you're pulling some kind of trick, and she's going to get me out, let me live with her or something."

"She won't even keep a dog."

Wesley frowned. "Go to hell, Lamar." He ground out the cigarette on the table.

V

Pearl, in her light blue Ford, turned into Mattie's driveway in front of Mattie. Mattie, driving the tan Plymouth that Paul bought just before he died, pulled in behind her and then up beside her so that Pearl could back out when she was ready to leave.

Mattie knew Pearl would ask her where she'd been. She'd go ahead and tell the truth—about visiting Wesley.

"Where you been?" asked Pearl, bending far left, then far right as they walked toward the back door.

"The prison."

Pearl raised an eyebrow. "They catch you writing bad checks?" She laughed.

"No." Once Mattie heard Pearl say to her gentle husband Carl, walking with a walker, after Carl said he'd live another fifteen to thirty years: "Unless you get shot in a whorehouse."

They stepped up and into the den. "I was visiting a prisoner," said Mattie. "Young fellow."

"What'd he do?"

"He says he didn't do nothing—that somebody put him up to it: stealing a car."

"You don't know who's going to do what these days," said Pearl, sitting on the couch. "Did you go with the Sunday school class?"

"No, I went by myself."

"You ought to be careful. There's mean boys out there." She reached into her pocketbook for her tin of snuff. "Mean enough to push biddies in the water."

"They got guards and all that. And as young as this boy is, I don't see how he could have got too mean yet. Course I don't know."

"They get mean young nowadays." Pearl placed a pinch of snuff in her lower lip. "I see you ain't got the bottom back to your rocker."

"Nope, nor to the kitchen chairs. I think Bill said tomorrow or Tuesday."

"How do you know this boy?"

"Well, he's some kin to the dogcatcher, and it hit me in Sunday school this morning for some reason. The scripture about the least of these. You know: 'When you've done something for the least of these my brethren, you've done it for me.' I thought that maybe if I took a piece of cake and pie out to that boy it would be like taking it to Jesus."

"Was it?"

"Well, I don't know. I never took no food to Jesus."

"Did it *seem* like the same?"

"No. He didn't look like Jesus, or talk like him."

"Well, you wouldn't expect him to if he stole a car."

"No, I don't guess you would. Listen, why don't you stay for supper. I can warm up my peas and corn, and stringbeans. Or . . ." Mattie stood and started over to the refrigerator. "I could fix us some bacon and eggs."

"I don't like mayonnaise."

Mattie stopped and turned. "Bacon and *eggs*."

"Oh. That'd be nice. I thought you said mayonnaise."

"No, bacon and eggs."

"I don't like mayonnaise."

"I know that. Which do you want—vegetables or bacon and eggs?"

"I don't care. Whatever's easiest." Pearl stood, walked into the kitchen.

"Here, sit on this one with the board," said Mattie.

Pearl walked around the table, bent over, carefully adjusted the board.

"Remember how we used to take water to the prisoners working on the road." She sat down.

"I remember. Striped suits. You know, it's a wonder Mama would let us go." Mattie went to the refrigerator for eggs. "This fellow had nice eyes, looked okay, but his teeth were rotten and his hair right stringy."

"Had the hives?"

"Nice *eyes*."

"Well, you just can't tell."

"He sure did enjoy that cake and pie."

"I reckon he did."

"You want a piece of toast and jelly while the bacon finishes?"

"Sure."

"I'm all out of preserves," said Mattie. "I wish I had a mess of strawberries. Alora bought a quart of the biggest, reddest, prettiest strawberries you ever seen at a yard sale last week. Cellophane stretched across the top. They were so pretty she brought them over to show me before she opened them. I told her the pretty ones were on top and the ugly ones were on the bottom, but she told me next day they were all pretty."

"You know, I been thinking it's about time we had another yard sale," said Pearl.

"Maybe so. How about some Saturday. Say, Saturday week. That'll give us time to plan."

"Okay, fine with me. We'll have it at my house. More traffic."

VI

After Pearl left, Mattie found her glasses in the top bureau drawer and sat down on the couch. She turned on the lamp, got her Bible from the table and looked in the concordance under "least." It wouldn't be in the Old Testament. Luke 16:10. She looked. No. 1 Corinthians 6:4. No, that wasn't it. Matthew, it seemed like—well, she would have to ask Martha or Carrie or Clarence Vernon.

Mattie got up to find the paper so she could see what was coming on TV. She shouldn't be watching television on Sunday night; she should be going to church. But she was afraid to drive after dark, and Alora and Finner didn't go, and she didn't want to have somebody pick her up. She looked in the TV section of the newspaper for any animal programs. None.

Well, then, no TV. She'd play and sing some hymns. She went to the piano, sat, leafed through the Broadman. Something simple to warm up on; something she could sing along with. Ah: key of G.

All hail the power of Jesus' name!
Let angels prostrate fall;
Bring forth the royal diadem,
And crown him Lord of all;
Bring forth the royal diadem,
And crown him Lord of all.

She thumbed through several pages. Here, here was one. "Love Lifted Me." B-flat. She played, remembering that it used to be Robert's and then Elaine's favorite.

Now Robert never went to church except occasionally he'd come home and go with Mattie at Easter or Christmas. She almost wished he wouldn't because it forced a question the next Sunday in Sunday school or church: "Where did you say Robert was going to church now?" And she'd say: "At the Lutheran church north of Listre." He had been there a few times.

Elaine hardly ever went to church. She was bitter. Maybe a little age would change her. She did go to that Unitarian place once in a while, but that was all.

The last time Mattie had tried to talk to Elaine about religion, Elaine had explained that the existence of the soul was not a given. She said it could all be in the brain: chemicals, nerve endings. But there was a *soul*, Mattie had protested. We have absolutely no evidence of that, said Elaine. Mattie had stood, walked from the kitchen table to the end table by the couch, and returned with her Bible and handed it to Elaine. Elaine had stood and said, "Mother, it is wonderful literature. There are beautiful stories all through it, and that's a wonderful achievement, a wonderful monument even, a monument to humanity, but Mother that's all it is. There is, in spite of this book, no clear evidence that we are dealing with anything but our imaginations."

Mattie had been horrified. It was as if Elaine had died and someone had returned in her place.

"To think otherwise," said Elaine, "I would have to be untrue to myself and I refuse to do that. You wouldn't want that, would you?"

To have a child think she was being *true* to herself and untrue to God was a magnificent and terrible problem.

After Elaine had gone home, Mattie thought over and over: why didn't I say you cannot be untrue to God and true to yourself because God is in all of us? Elaine couldn't have had a good answer for that. But Mattie had only stared at Elaine, unable to say anything, feeling tears swell in her eyes, hating that she could only cry rather than say the exact right thing that would clear the blinders from her own daughter's heart—bring her to Jesus, bring Jesus to her. She had done everything she knew to do—sent Elaine to Bible school every summer of her life, to church every Sunday and Sunday night, to . . . everywhere she could, and read and told her Bible stories over and over and over.

VII

At midnight on Friday night, Wesley stood on a cinder-block step and knocked on the door of Lamar's mobile home.

He knocked again, louder.

A light came on. The door opened. Lamar stood there in his underwear.

"You got a girl with you?" asked Wesley.

"Wesley! What the hell? No, I ain't."

Wesley tried to open the screen door. It was hooked.

"Wait a minute," said Lamar. "Did you escape?"

"You goddamn right. Open the door."

"Wesley, they'll fry my ass if they find you here."

"I'm leaving for South Carolina tomorrow. Tomorrow night. Myrtle Beach. This guy Blake Bumgartner is getting a car and is going to pick me up at Creek Junction behind the 7-Eleven. It's all set up. I just—"

"Listen, Wesley. I don't want to know about it."

"I just need something to eat and that belt and stuff I sent. Maybe a shirt and a pair of pants. They won't know I'm gone until tomorrow morning. Let me in." Wesley looked left and right. He wiped his nose with the back of his hand. "Let me in, man."

Lamar unhooked the screen, stepped back.

Wesley came in. "Boy I'm glad to get out of that place. No way they'll *ever* catch me, man. Ever."

"When they find out you're gone they'll come here."

"I'll be gone. They'll find out I'm gone at breakfast. I'll be out of here by then." Wesley looked around. "Listen, if you're so damned scared just loan me thirty dollars and take me down to the Landmark Motel."

"I ain't got thirty dollars." Lamar looked through a window. "Don't they do some kind of midnight check?"

"Hell, no. It ain't prison, it's a goddamned correction center."

"Well, you sure as hell can't just walk out. How'd you get out?"

"Secret."

"Good. Listen, I can't keep you here."

"Well, I got to sleep somewhere. Goddamn, Lamar, I'm family, man. Shit. Where does that old woman live?"

"What old woman?"

"The one might be my grandma—with the cake and stuff."

"Oh, Mrs. Rigsbee. She lives in Listre. Why?"

Wesley leaned against the sink, eyed the dirty dishes.

"I told Blake I'd have some of the best cake he ever eat—from my grandma. Man, that was the best cake I ever eat."

"Don't get any ideas about stealing cake, Wesley."

"I ain't. I ain't." Wesley sat down in a chair on several newspapers.

Lamar walked over and sat on the couch. "Yeah, she can flat cook, all right. I'm supposed to take her a well-house roof tomorrow."

"Can you get me a big hunk of that cake?"

"Hell no, I can't do that. Listen, you got to get out of here."

"Where does she keep her cake?"

"Hell, I don't know. Why? Wesley, don't go steal none of her *cake*. Listen, ah, it's warm outside. I'll pull the truck out behind the shop and you can take my sleeping bag and sleep in the truck bed. If the law comes I'll turn on the light and them speakers out there and you sneak off or something."

"Okay. Hell, I can do that. But I could just sleep on the couch it seems like to me," said Wesley.

Lamar stood. "No way. You sleep in the truck. I'll get the sleeping bag. If they catch you, you tell them you got it out of the truck and never saw me. Here—bug spray."

"Where's my belt and that bracelet and stuff?"

"I'll get it." Lamar went to his bedroom and came back with a manila envelope and a paper sack. Inside the envelope was Wesley's thick leather belt with "Wesley" carved across the back, an Indian-made silver ring and bracelet with light blue settings, and a leather necklace. In the sack were a pair of trousers and two T-shirts.

While Lamar was moving the truck, Wesley picked up the telephone and dialed. "Patricia? This is Wesley . . . *Wes*ley . . . Yeah, I busted out. Me and Blake planned it and he'll be out tomorrow night . . . I'm sorry, I thought you'd be up. Well listen, why don't you come over to Lamar's in the morning? . . . Yeah, the trailer. We'll go on a picnic or something . . . Okay, good night . . . Moochie moo you, too."

"Moochie *moo?*" Lamar stepped inside.

"Don't worry about it."

"Was that Patricia?"

"Yeah. She might come over tomorrow."

"Y'all are going somewhere, ain't you?"

"Picnic or something."

Wesley slept behind Lamar's shop in the truck bed. Saturday morning after helping Lamar load the well top into the truck bed he asked if he could see inside Lamar's shop for a few minutes. Lamar let him in. Wesley stood in the doorway. Across the back wall hung tools—several makes of the same tool were hung side by side in descending sizes. There were five hammers, four wood saws, three hacksaws, six paint brushes, adjustable wrenches, chisels. A long table held a plane, other tools, small jars and cigar boxes of screws, nuts, bolts, and nails. Along one side wall was a table with a lathe, a clamp, electric saw, and electric file.

"Why don't you keep your trailer this neat?" said Wesley. "Them dishes stunk."

"Don't worry about it. Listen, I got to get going."

"Well," said Wesley, backing out of the door. "It's a nice one."

"Yeah, I got a lot of money in it," said Lamar.

As Lamar was driving away, Patricia pulled up in her Camaro.

Wesley got in beside her. "Follow Lamar, but stay way back so he don't see you."

As Lamar turned into Mattie's driveway and drove behind the house, Particia pulled over on the roadside and Wesley got out.

"You stay right here," he said to Patricia. "I'll be back inside ten minutes with the best pound cake you ever eat in your life."

Wesley walked along the road toward Mattie's house. On the side of the house facing him was the porch. The screen door to the side porch was in the front. While they were out back at the well house he could walk from the road straight across the front yard, up to the porch, into the kitchen, find that pound cake, walk out, and back down to the car. Blake would not believe how good it was—he'd talk about it all the way through South Carolina and into Myrtle Beach, where they were going to get a job on a fishing boat or tourist boat or something. Blake had worked down there before. Warm year round. Lots of honeys.

Wesley walked past the house and saw Lamar's truck in the backyard. Some man was helping Lamar unload the well top. Perfect. Perfect timing. He turned, walked back a ways, then across the yard and up the four steps to the screen door. He looked around, grabbed the door handle and pulled. It was *hooked*. What the *hell*? He rattled the door. Loose. He looked for the hook: there. It was a simple hook, without one of those gadgets. Easy. He pulled a book of matches from his pocket, opened the cover, inserted it down low in the crack of the door, and started sliding it upward.

In the backyard, Lamar and Finner had just finished fitting the well-house top in place and Finner had started painting it.

"Let me run in and check my roast," said Mattie. "You're going to be able to stay for a bite to eat, ain't you, Lamar."

"Yeah, I am."

I wish he would say, "Yes ma'am," thought Mattie. "Finner, why don't you and Alora eat a bite with us? I got plenty."

"I think Alora's going shopping."

"Well, you can eat with us. Let me go check that roast."

Wesley had worked the open matchbook cover up to about one inch below the hook. He heard footsteps inside. The house door opened. Wesley instinctively knocked.

Mattie squinted. Who was that? "How do you do?" she said. She walked across the porch. Who was that? "Why you're the young man from the prison: Wesley. I been thinking about you!"

"I been thinking 'bout you too." Wesley looked down the road toward Patricia's car. The sun reflected off the front windshield. The matchbook did not move. It was stuck in the crack. He turned it loose. "What you doing?" he said.

"Fixing my well top. Lamar's in back. You looking for him?"

"Yeah. Looking for Lamar."

"Let me unhook this." Mattie unhooked the screen. The matchbook fell to the floor. "What's that?"

"Looks like a matchbook." He bent, picked it up, and handed it to Mattie.

"What are you doing out of the RC?"

"They let me out for a few days—on leave. We get leave every once in a while."

"Well. That's good. Good. Come on out back. Lamar will be happy to see you."

They started through the house.

"Ah, listen, Mrs., ah, I forgot your name."

Mattie stopped and turned around. They were in the kitchen. "Mrs. Rigsbee."

"Yeah. Let me run tell my girlfriend . . . ah, she was going to, ah, shop downtown some when I came on looking for Lamar. Let me run tell her I found him. I'll be right back."

"Okay, we'll be in the backyard. You and her can stay for a bite to eat if you want to. I got plenty: a roast beef. We're going to eat kind of early."

"That'll be fine." Damn, I could use some roast beef.

Patricia sat with her elbow out of the window. She had been counting the dots under the numbers on the speedometer. She saw Wesley walking toward her rapidly. He came up to the window, rested his hand on the outside rearview mirror. "You want to eat?" he said.

"Eat?"

"Yeah, eat."

"I thought you were going to get some cake?"

"*Eat.* Eat food. Roast beef. I ain't eat in two days."

"What if they announce that you escaped on TV and radio?"

"They won't. Not for escaping from the YMRC. Let's go." Wesley got in the car. "Drive on up there."

Lamar waited on the side porch. Finner was in the backyard painting the wood of the well top white. Mattie was in the kitchen.

Lamar walked to the screen door, opened it and stood on the steps waiting for Wesley and Patricia, who were walking up across the yard. When they approached he hissed, "Wesley, what the *hell* are you doing here?"

"I come to eat."

"You're going to get us all in trouble—harboring a criminal or something."

"He ain't a criminal," said Patricia.

"You tell that to the highway patrol."

The three of them walked into the kitchen where Mattie was peeling potatoes. "I thought I better do a few more potatoes," she said. "You don't want to run out of potatoes."

Wesley looked around for a silver chest.

"You all sit down over there if you will," said Mattie. "Turn on that TV." She turned around, saw Patricia in the doorway. Her knife stopped on a potato. "Oh, good morning. You must be Wesley's . . . girlfriend?" All that makeup, thought Mattie.

"Yes, ma'am, I am." Patricia crossed her arms, leaned against the door frame between the porch and kitchen.

Lamar and Wesley walked over and sat down in the den.

Jesus wouldn't have a girlfriend, Mattie thought. Or maybe he would. Why wouldn't he? He was a normal human being at the same time he was God. Mary Magdalene, wadn't it. Maybe. She'd never got that straight.

"Need some help?" asked Patricia.

"Oh, no. I can get it all . . . Well, you might put ice in those glasses. It's in the freezer. The lemon's right over there . . . Put in a lot of ice. I like a lot of ice in my tea."

Wesley turned on the TV. He and Lamar sat on the couch.

Elaine drove up in the backyard.

Finner was still painting the well top.

Back inside, Wesley picked up a pair of tweezers from the end table. "Lamar," he said.

Lamar looked.

Wesley pretended to pluck his eyelashes with the tweezers. "'Member when I did that?"

"Yeah, I remember. I remember when you stuffed Cheerios up your nose and sneezed them all over the place, too."

"Patricia, did you hear that?" said Wesley.

"What?"

Elaine walked in through the back door. First, she saw a teenager with heavy eyeshadow pouring tea, a job always reserved for her when she was home. Then she saw Lamar and Wesley. "Hello," she said, looking at Wesley.

Wesley, looking at Elaine, said to Patricia: "About how I stuffed Cheerios up my nose and then sneezed them all over the place."

"I beg your pardon?" said Elaine.

"I was talking to Patricia."

"Oh, of course."

Mattie, wiping her hands on her apron, met Elaine at the end of the counter separating the kitchen and dining room. They stood face to face, Elaine trying to move on into the kitchen away from Wesley and Lamar in the den.

"Let me introduce everybody," said Mattie.

"Could we turn down the TV?" asked Elaine.

Mattie stepped to the TV and turned it down. "This is Lamar, the dogcatcher, and his nephew Wesley, and over here, Patricia. You heard me talk about the dogcatcher."

"He was here when I was, Saturday."

"That's right. He got me out of the chair, you know. Y'all, this is Elaine, my daughter."

Wesley, picking his nose, looked back at the television. Elaine looked exactly like one of the women that came to the YMRC and asked thousands and thousands of questions which left him feeling like somebody had grabbed his gonads, gently swung them out and looked all around behind them. He wished Elaine would go on into the living room. Or back where she came from.

"I think we might need the leaf in the table," said Mattie.

"I'm not sure I can stay," said Elaine.

"Why not?"

"Well, I . . ."

"I got plenty—a whole roast beef; and I just peeled some extra potatoes. And a whole cabbage, plus a whole new pound cake on the back porch."

"Let me see the pound cake," said Elaine.

"What?"

"Let me *see* the pound cake." Elaine nudged Mattie toward the back porch.

"What is it?" asked Mattie, on the back porch.

"Who are all these people?"

"They're people."

"They look like riffraff."

"Riffraff?"

"They look like riffraff."

"Lamar is a nice-looking boy—if he'd remember to take off his hat in the house."

"That hat looks like it went through the Civil War. And what about his friend?"

"Wesley, his nephew."

"*He* doesn't look like a 'nice boy.'"

"He's not. He's one of the least of these my brethren."

"He's what?"

"You know, from the Bible, one of the least of these my brethren. Like Jesus said. He's had a hard life."

"Mother, are you feeling okay?"

"I'm just feeding him. I ain't adopting him."

"Mother, these people—"

"I got to get to the meal." Mattie went back inside. Elaine stood for a moment, then walked to the screen door of the porch. She looked through the screen, studied how it matted the world outside, how if she got close to it, it blurred. She will never die, she thought. She'll always have a meal going which will not turn her loose.

Mattie came back to the door. "Come in here and help me with this table leaf. We need it in."

Around the table sat Elaine, Wesley, Patricia, Lamar, and Finner. Mattie's chair was empty because she was still tending to the stove and putting food on the table. Elaine was talking to Finner—asking him about Alora, the children and grandchildren. Elaine had always disliked Finner, but here, at this table, with these other people, she suddenly found him quite attractive, likable.

"The biscuits will be just another minute," said Mattie, closing the stove.

"Why don't you sit down and eat," said Elaine. "I can tend to the biscuits."

"Let's say the blessing," said Mattie, "so y'all can go ahead and get started. Wesley, say the blessing, son."

"Do what?"

"Say the blessing." Mattie wanted to see if he knew a blessing to say.

Wesley eyed Lamar, who bowed his head and closed his eyes. Wesley had heard blessings in farmer movies, and in real life when the church people served watermelon at the orphanage.

"Thank God for this food and us being free and all the other good things in life. Amen."

"Amen. Y'all go ahead," said Mattie, still standing, waiting for the biscuits.

"Mother, I think we have enough bread anyway with this cornbread and these rolls."

"A few biscuits won't hurt."

Elaine said to Wesley: "I'll have some of that; we generally pass things around, from one person to the other."

"Oh." Wesley eyed Lamar. Lamar was busy with the creamed potatoes.

"I'm going to go ahead and take them out," said Mattie. "If you like them real brown, you're out of luck. Anybody like them real brown?"

"I do," said Wesley.

"Well, let's see, why don't I just . . ." Mattie pulled the pan from the oven, dropped it onto the counter from about two feet up so the biscuits would break from the bottom. Patricia jumped.

"Why don't I just break off about three and put them back in for Wesley?" She put three biscuits back in the oven.

"Mother. Why don't you just bring the biscuits over here and sit down and eat?"

Mattie set biscuits on the table, sat down, took a bowl Finner handed her. "Where are you headed today?" she asked Elaine.

"Chapel Hill," said Elaine. "There's a conference on women's issues—women in prison."

"You've got to be one hell of a mean woman to go to prison," said Wesley, his mouth full of potatoes.

Elaine watched to see where Wesley placed his roll. Ah, on the table near his plate. He hadn't put his napkin in his lap. He hadn't known to pass the food. This would be instructive. "Well, I think—"

"Most of the women in prison killed somebody," said Wesley.

"Well, they end up there many times because of the kind of life forced on them," said Elaine.

"Stuff ain't forced on all of them."

"I'd say a significant number—many are forced to stay in the home."

"Not all of them are forced." Wesley looked at the stove. "I bet my biscuits are about ready."

"Oh, Lord," said Mattie. She stood, went to the stove, opened the oven door, got out Wesley's three biscuits, put them on a small dish which she set in front of his plate. Wesley picked one up, took a bite, and placed it on the table next to his roll.

"It's hard work at home," said Patricia. "It's like life in the hard lane. My mama goes crazy sometimes."

"Where do you live?" asked Mattie.

"Between here and Bristol Lake," said Patricia.

I'd like to know where those two spent the night, thought Elaine.

Lamar was beginning to worry about the police finding Wesley—somehow tracing him to this house.

"What's your last name?" Finner asked Patricia.

"Boles."

"What does your daddy do?"

"He split about six years ago."

"Split? . . . Split what? Wood?"

"Split. Hauled ass. Left."

What a foul mouth, thought Mattie. I thought she looked a little washed out.

"Oh, I see," said Finner. I wish Alora could have heard that, he thought.

"I got four brothers and sisters," said Patricia, "and they drive mama crazy."

"That's what I mean," said Elaine. "They get put in that position. You don't see men staying home with kids, going crazy."

"Men have to work," said Wesley. "Somebody does. Anyway, it takes a sorry man to do woman's work."

"Well," said Elaine. "Well. Well. This is an old, tiresome argument." Her therapist had warned her about getting hooked into arguments with immature people. This was a good test. The problem was seeing it before you got involved. She stabbed one, then another butterbean, and with her teeth pulled them off her fork onto her tongue, let them rest there for a few seconds before chewing them lightly. They were good, tasty butterbeans. The older she got, the more she wished she could cook like her mother.

"This is good, Mrs. Rigsbee," said Lamar.

"She is a good cook," said Wesley to Patricia. "She brought me that cake and pie I told you about."

"When?" said Elaine.

"The other day," said Wesley.

"Where?"

Wesley looked at Mattie who was reaching for the bowl of butterbeans, not answering.

"Who needs some more butterbeans?" said Mattie, standing. "We got plenty."

"Where did you meet?" asked Elaine.

"Wesley was out at the YMRC until he got out on leave," said Mattie. "When? Last day or two?" she asked Wesley.

"Yesterday," said Wesley. He smiled at Lamar. "I'll take some more of that over there please."

I wish we could do something about those teeth, thought Mattie.

VIII

Saturday night Patricia drove Wesley to the 7-Eleven at Creek Junction, where he was supposed to meet Blake Bumgartner. Wesley held three pieces of pound cake wrapped separately: one for him, one for Patricia, and one for Blake. But Blake didn't show up.

They sat in Patricia's car around back, where they were supposed to meet him. "We'll wait another fifteen minutes," said Wesley. "He screwed it all up somehow."

"What are you going to do if he don't show up?" asked Patricia.

"Eat the cake."

"I mean after that. I got to go home."

"Hell, I don't know. Go to Lamar's, I reckon. I don't know." Wesley thought about Mattie placing bowls of good hot food on the table in front of him. "Maybe I can go to Mrs. Rigsbee's." He envisioned the extra room she probably had—a soft warm room with a soft bed and a big fluffy pillow and big warm chairs he could sit in and watch stuff on a little portable TV that might be in there. "I'll go to her house. She came to see me first. She might be my grandma." Wesley looked at Patricia. "Did you know that?"

"No, I didn't."

They waited a while longer, but Blake didn't come.

"Take me to Mrs. Rigsbee's," said Wesley. "And we might as well go ahead and eat this piece of cake, too. Hell, I'm glad he didn't come."

When Wesley opened the car door and started up the walk to Mattie Rigsbee's brick ranch he felt relieved to be away from Patricia. She looked all right, but she had begun to get on his nerves. She didn't talk much and she had to check in at home about every two hours.

It was 9:30. There was a light on in the living room and somebody was playing the piano. What kind of music was that? One of them hymns. When he got to the door he heard Mattie singing.

Yes, we'll gather at the river,
The beautiful, the beautiful river;
Gather with the saints at the river
That flows by the throne of God.

Mattie heard the knock. Who in the world? At this time of night. Saturday night. Who could it be? She turned on the porch light at the door, and looked out through the glass. Well, my goodness. Wesley. "Come in," she said, opening the door.

Wesley stepped in and looked around.

"What you got there?" said Mattie, looking at the paper bag.

"Few clothes."

"Oh? . . . Well, have a seat. You just in the neighborhood?"

"Yeah. Have you got a extra room?" he said, sitting down in Mattie's swan-neck rocker.

"Well . . ."

Wesley's hands were on the chair arms. He put them in his lap and then back on the chair arms. "I need a place to sleep for one night before I go see this buddy of mine. Lamar's got company, and I thought maybe . . ."

"Yes, well, yes. I suppose you can stay in Robert's room." Mattie sat down on the couch. "When is your leave over?"

"I got about nine more days."

"You need to take a bath or anything?"

"You got a bathtub?"

"Shower or bath."

"I ain't ever had a bath."

"Never had a bath?"

"I always had showers." Wesley thought about the commercial he'd seen on TV where a woman had soap bubbles up to her neck. "You got any of them soap bubbles?"

"No, no soap bubbles. But listen, let me tell you something: I got to get up and go to church tomorrow morning and if you want to stay here then you're going to have to go to church too. I can't just leave you here by yourself."

"Why?"

"Because I'm inviting you to go to church with me and if you're going to stay here and use my bathtub . . . Have you ever been to church?"

"I been *by* them, seen them on TV, slept in one one time, but I ain't never been in one when they were doing the thing."

Mattie saw before her a dry, dying plant which needed water up through the roots—a pale boy with rotten teeth who needed the cool nourishing water of hymns sung to God, of kind people speaking to him, asking him how things were going, the cool water of clean people, clean children, of old people being held by the arm and helped up a flight of stairs, old people who looked with thanks up into the eyes of their helpers, of young and old people sitting together for one purpose: to worship their Maker, to worship Jesus, to do all that together and to care for each other and to read and sing and talk together about God and Jesus and the Bible. That's what this young man needed. That would bring color to his cheeks, a robustness to his bearing. That would do it. That could give him some life and spirit. He seemed smart enough. And, since he hadn't been to church, then he was lost; this could be his first step on the road to salvation.

"Well, I want you to go with me in the morning. We'll get up and I'll fix you a little breakfast, get dinner started, then we'll go to Sunday school. You can go in the Young People's Department or you can go in with me. Then we'll go to church. You can sit with me. Then we'll come on back and have some pork chops and vegetables and so forth and so on."

Wesley looked around. "Okay. I'll go."

"Good. Let me get out a clean washrag and towel for you and you can take a bath. It's about my bedtime."

Mattie walked down the hallway and into the bathroom.

Wesley looked around for something to steal.

Mattie came back in a few minutes. "The bathroom's ready if you want to go ahead. Come on and I'll show you where you can sleep."

Wesley followed Mattie into Robert's room. He looked around—twin beds, a desk, a chest of drawers. He'd check out the drawers to the desk and chest. Might be something in there worth a few bucks. Something she wouldn't miss. If he found a box of silver somewhere, he'd take about one-third of it. She wouldn't miss part of it maybe.

"I got a few things to do in the kitchen," said Mattie. "You go ahead and take a bath. The bathroom's right back there in the hall. Do you have any pajamas?"

"No, I don't wear them."

"Well, I'll get you out a pair of Robert's. Use that bed over there and I'll wake you up in the morning about seven. How do you like your eggs?"

"I don't care. Fresh."

"They'll be fresh enough. How about scrambled?"

"That'll be okay."

"Well, good night. Make yourself at home."

Mattie left. Wesley opened a cigar box on the dresser.

Inside were small medals and pins, papers. He read from the medals: Listre Elementary Declamation 1954–55; RA; State NFSM. He wondered if they could be melted down. Nobody would want them like they were. Why hadn't that guy, Robert, melted them down? Two pocket-knives, a Kennedy half-dollar key ring: hell, he could use that—when he got some keys. He pocketed the key ring, one of the knives. What was in the little cloth bag? Marbles. The papers—Grade 3, Citizenship Certificate. Math Certificate. Sunday School Attendance. English Certificate, Grade 6. Damn, this guy must have been a genius. Why was he saving all this stuff? Or maybe *she* was saving it. Maybe it was how she remembered him— came in and looked through it once in a while.

Wesley put his hand in his pocket, held the key ring and the pocketknife there. She would miss them. He ought to be different with her; she was probably his grandma. She even favored him a little bit, around the eyes. He could tell.

He put the knife and key ring back and closed the box. He'd keep the pen and pencil he'd gotten from the living room, though. People were always losing pens and pencils one way or another.

In the kitchen, Mattie got out the pots and pans she would need in the morning. And the big frying pan. Well, wasn't this a good chance. That boy needed a bath. He smelled a little bit. Which is what you'd expect of one of the least of these my brethren. If he was all cleaned up she wouldn't need to do anything for him. He needed to go back to the RC after his leave as a better young man inside and outside—better than he was before.

The phone rang. Who in the world could that be? It was ten o'clock.

"Hello?"

"Mother, you gone to bed?" It was Robert.

"No, I'm just getting things ready for in the morning."

"Well, listen. Would it be all right if I brought somebody by for you to meet tomorrow?"

"A woman?"

"Yes. Somebody I've dated a couple of times and I thought maybe—"

"Why yes, of course. Bring her to dinner. What's her name?"

"Laurie. Laurie Thomas."

"That'd be fine. Somebody else might be here, too. A visitor. How old is Laurie?"

"How *old* is she?"

"I just wondered."

"She's thirty-five or so. Why do you always have to ask me that?"

"I just wondered." Three, four, or five years to have children, thought Mattie. Well, that's good. "Bring her on. Can y'all be here by 12:30?"

"Oh yeah. We'll see you then."

"Okay. Bye-bye."

Well, she'd get another two pork chops out of the freezer. She had plenty. This would be nice. A woman. Robert bringing home a woman. It would be all right for Wesley to be there. She would feed them all. They would all together enjoy her food. She could find out about the young woman. But now, after this long, she figured just about anybody would be okay for Robert, even if she didn't approve entirely. Wesley would be clean and dressed up a little bit. Maybe if she got him up in time, she could cut his hair, before she took him to church.

Wesley stood nude in the bathroom, his clothes piled on the commode top. The water steamed as it poured into the tub. No bubble stuff. Maybe if he poured in some of that shampoo. He removed the cap from the plastic bottle, squeezed some into the water. It didn't do much. He squeezed some more. And more. There. That's the way it was supposed to do. It was making suds. He bent over and put his hand in the water. Just right. Then it wasn't filling up anymore. The water was going out that little hole. He picked up a small cake of soap, felt until he found the hole, and jammed in the soap. He would fill the tub right up to the brim. God, look at those suds. He wished he had a cold beer. He stepped to the mirror and looked at himself. He opened the medicine cabinet. Nothing much in there. Band-Aids, Vicks VapoRub, and a tube of something. Shit, he could sneak out after she went to bed and walk down to the intersection where those stores were. There was a Pizza Inn and some other stores down there. He closed the medicine cabinet door. He'd buy a couple of beers. Hell, six. And some cigarettes. He needed a cigarette. Now that he was settled in for the night he could do a little celebrating. The water suddenly overflowed and ran across the floor around his feet.

"Shit." He took a long stride toward the faucet, bent and turned it off, stuck his hand into the water. Just right.

He stepped into the tub. With hands on both sides of the tub, elbows extended, he sat down in the warm water. The tub sloshed over again. Suds and water washed down onto the floor; "Wups," he said, glancing at the floor; then, "Goddamn, that feels good," as he looked up to the ceiling, and slid downward—pushing out another wave of water and suds—so that only his head and knees were above water.

Mattie stood just outside the bathroom door on the soaking wet hall rug; she heard the water splash over onto the floor; she heard Wesley talking to himself.

"Young man, there will be no cussing in this house," she said.

"I ain't in the house, I'm in the tub."

"Yes you are too in this house and what in the world have you done? Overflowed the tub?"

"Yeah, a little bit got on the floor. I didn't mean to."

Lord have mercy, thought Mattie. I've overdone it. I'll have to clean up and I don't know what all. But. But it's for only one night. And this boy is needy. That's what he is: needy. If anybody is needy it's this boy. He would benefit. He would be nourished in body and spirit. The floor would dry up. "Listen," she said to Wesley. "I used to do a little barbering. How 'bout if I give you a haircut in the morning?"

"A haircut? Okay." Damn. Wesley wanted a diamond, too, to put in his left ear, but he figured he'd better not mention that to Mattie. Maybe she had an old diamond ring in her bedroom somewhere. He'd have to figure out a time to get in there. When she was cooking breakfast. God, this bath felt good. Damn thing made him light as hell, made his body light, lifted him up. He pushed his pelvis upward. There it was—a little wharf-rat head, like a little live being with him in the tub. The suds had about disappeared and the water had turned a light gray.

I won't worry about the water, thought Mattie, backing off from the door. It'll dry up. I won't worry about it. I'll check his room one more time. She went into the room. I wonder if he has any clean underwear. I'll check in the paper bag, Food Lion bag. They're stronger than those Piggly Wigglys, she thought. She slowly unrolled the bag. Yep, there on top was a pair of white jockey shorts just like Robert wore. And there was a pair of right nice khaki pants. And there . . . what was that? Wasn't that her . . . it *was*. Her gold pen and pencil set from the living room. He'd stolen them! She reached in and got them. Well, of all things! And she was being so good to him. And he was stealing from her. How could he? That young whippersnapper. She would have to jerk a knot in his neck. She'd have to shake him up. She'd walk in on him in the bathtub. Tell him a thing or two. She wouldn't embarrass him—his privates would be under water. She'd scare him. By golly, she wasn't going to roll over and play dead to a young man who was *stealing* off her under her very nose.

Wesley was slowly pushing his hips upward again.

Mattie marched toward the bathroom door. The wetness in the rug was spreading. Lord, that would be days drying up. She burst into the bathroom.

Wesley bolted upright; his mouth dropped open. "*What the hell you want?*"

Mattie stopped suddenly. But her feet kept going on the wet floor. Catching the sink with one hand, holding the pen and pencil over her head with the other, she slid down onto the floor.

"What the hell?" said Wesley. "You scared the shit out of me! You hurt?"

They stared at each other—Mattie sitting on the floor, Wesley in the tub.

"I don't think so." Mattie held up the pen and pencil. "Look at that. You stole my gold pen and pencil from the drawer in the living room. The very idea!"

"I didn't steal them. I . . . You all right? Damn, you looked like you was sliding into second base." Wesley threw back his head and laughed. "You 'bout busted your butt is what you did."

"Well, what did you do, if you didn't steal them?" Mattie turned over onto her hands and knees, and then holding onto the sink with one hand, pulled up slowly from the wet floor. Standing, she held out the pen and pencil. "These."

"I just borrowed them to write a letter to my daddy before I left. Tell him where I was going. You all right?"

"Yes, I'm all right. You had the pen *and* the pencil. You didn't need the pen *and* the pencil."

"I thought one might give out. You shouldn't be standing there watching me like this."

"I should be if you stole my gold pen and pencil."

"No you shouldn't either. I didn't steal them."

Mattie shifted her weight. She wasn't hurt one bit—didn't even land hard. Maybe he was telling the truth.

He did write letters. She'd seen the one to Lamar. "Listen, you mop up this floor when you get finished. There's a mop in the kitchen pantry."

"I can do that. I didn't know the thing was going to run over. Listen, you shouldn't be looking at me."

"Well, when you get through and get your clothes on you mop up the floor." Mattie slowly backed out of the door and closed it. Well, maybe he was telling the truth. Even if he wasn't, she still had her obligations toward him. He was one of the least of these my brethren whether he stole or not. In fact, she thought, if he was a thief then he was even more one of the least of these. "It's about time for you to get out, ain't it."

She heard a faucet turn on. "Soon's I warm it up a little. I'll be out in a minute. You go ahead to bed. I'll be out in a minute."

Mattie walked into the kitchen to check everything one last time. Thank goodness that fall hadn't hurt her. She felt her hips. She was okay. She looked around. The pots and pans were out. The pork chops were out of the freezer. She could go ahead and make her tea before she went to bed so she wouldn't have to do that in the morning. Give her a little more time to cut Wesley's hair. What if he *had* been stealing her pen and pencil? She remembered stealing fifty cents one time—when she was a little girl—from the table beside her uncle Scott's big green chair. Maybe Wesley *was* going to write a letter. She'd see if he wrote a letter. She'd ask him before he left.

She started to her bedroom, passed the bathroom. He was still in there. "Are you going to stay in there all night?"

"No. I'll be out in a minute. This feels good."

He certainly needed a good hot bath, Mattie thought. She went on into her bedroom and closed the door. She opened the door and shouted, "Be sure you mop up that floor."

"I will. I will." Wesley pulled out the stopper and watched the level of gray water slowly drop. It was going out pretty fast. Sometimes it stood in the showers at the YMRC.

The level was down now, the water was cool; he'd fill it up with hot water. He stuck the stopper back in, then leaned his head against the back of the tub, sliding down until he was comfortable. He closed his eyes almost all the way so that he could see the overhead light through his eyelashes. His feet were getting hot; he stirred them so the warm water would spread throughout the bath. Maybe he could stay with Mrs. Rigsbee a few days. They'd never think to look for him living with an old woman. They didn't know she might be his grandma. He picked up his hand from out of the water and held it above his eye so water dropped onto his eyelashes. He squinted. Thousands of tiny little rainbows. He again remembered the time he pulled his eyelashes out with a tweezer. Why the hell had he done that? He remembered how each time his eyelid had stretched way, way out. He'd wanted to clean his face up like John Sterky who rode a motorcycle with his older brother. John didn't have any eyelashes or eyebrows, but had hair on his head. John wore a leather collar and silver Indian jewelry with light blue stones. Wesley had wanted to be just like John. Instead he'd just spent some class period, third or fourth maybe, pulling out his eyelashes one by one and Erma Tarkington had seen it and reported it and he'd been called to the office and written up as a "disturbed youth."

Thousands of tiny rainbows. The water was hot all around him. He leaned up and turned the faucet off. When he leaned back water splashed over the edge of the tub onto the floor. He rested his head against the back of the tub, sunk down a little bit. A little more water washed over the edge of the tub. He relaxed. His body almost floated. It was so warm. He picked one tiny dot and followed it around and around. The swirling slowed.

Mattie, in her pajamas, sat at her dresser and squirted a bit of Jergens lotion into her hand. She rubbed her hands together. She heard the water swash around in the tub. It was a good sound in a way. She wasn't alone like she'd been for four years. Or was it five? Five. Well, Elaine had stayed for several nights after Paul died. And Robert stayed over about twice a year. But here was an outsider in her house at night, sharing her home, her bath—someone who was needy. Of course Elaine and Robert were needy in their own way. They needed a husband and a wife. She opened the jar of Pond's cold cream and took out some on the tips of her fingers. She rubbed her hands together and rubbed the cold cream on her face: cheeks, forehead, chin. She would check one more time to see if he was out. And then she wouldn't worry anymore. It was 10:30. She needed to get to sleep. Tomorrow would be a big day.

Wesley was a black balloon floating up, up, up. A ceiling of some sort was coming down, down, down. They met; he bounced repeatedly off the ceiling: knock, knock, knock.

"Isn't it about time for you to get out?"

He awoke. Where the hell was he? He bolted up and looked at the water around him. It came to him: cake, food, warmth. "I'm getting out now. I went to sleep."

"You could drown with all that water you got drawed in there."

"I won't drown." He stood slowly. His body felt so heavy. He grabbed a towel.

"Well, I'm going to bed," said Mattie. "Good night."

"Good night." Wesley stood in the water, looking at the water and sang John Prine:

Blow up your TV, throw away your paper.
Move to the country, build you a home.

He stepped out of the tub and began to dry off. He was warm all over.

"Do you like grits?" Mattie asked from the hall.

"I like anything but tomatoes."

"Good *home-grown* tomatoes?"

"Any kind."

"Lord, there's nothing better in the world. It's so good with bacon. I'm going to have some."

"Eat anything you want." He looked at the door. Why the hell didn't she leave him alone. "Why don't you go on to bed."

"I am. Good night."

"Good night." He believed he would go on to bed himself. He was too tired to go to the Pizza Inn. He pictured the bed waiting. The sheets would probably be white, clean, starched.

In her bedroom Mattie turned back her covers. She stepped to her closed bedroom door and opened it slightly. He might need something in the night, she thought. Might get up and not be able to find the light or something.

IX

Mattie awoke at 4:00 A.M., got up, went barefooted to Wesley's door and pushed on it gently—to see if he was all right, if he was covered up, if she could hear him breathing. If he wasn't covered, she'd cover him. But his door was shut tight. She decided to leave him. She might startle him. She returned to her bed and went back to sleep.

At 5:30 she got up again, put on her housecoat and sweater for breakfast. It was dark outside. She followed the light from her bedroom lamp down the hall—and into the kitchen, and turned on the kitchen light—a coiled fluorescent bulb which had lasted over ten years.

Everything was ready to go. Bacon first, started in a cold frying pan, which was waiting.

What could she have that was special, different? A cantaloupe off the porch—no, she had some sliced in the refrigerator. Molasses? Biscuits? She'd ask him if he knew how to stick his finger in a biscuit, then pour in molasses. When she was growing up there were times when all they'd had for a meal was a biscuit, molasses, and cheese. They'd never been without, but times had gotten thin. She remembered when at school the other children had white bread sandwiches and she and Pearl and her brothers had only biscuits.

At 6:45, with all the food ready, and the table set, Mattie went to Wesley's room to wake him up. She opened the door. Morning light was in the room. Wesley was on his side, facing her, asleep, his arm out over the cover.

She decided not to touch him. He might jump all over the place. "Breakfast's ready."

His eyes opened but he didn't move. Then he jerked up onto his elbow and looked around, stared at her, recognized her. "Damn, I didn't wake up a single time."

"Good. Biscuits are coming out of the oven. Be in the kitchen in five minutes if you want them warm." She walked out.

Wesley stared at a glass knob on the dresser. Warm biscuits?

"I'll be there," he said. He got out of bed, put on his khaki slacks and a T-shirt and started to the kitchen. He stopped by the bathroom. Damn, water still on the floor. Oh, well.

In the kitchen, Mattie was waiting for him with a mop

in her hand. "You were supposed to mop the bathroom floor last night."

"Oh yeah. Right. I was so tired I forgot."

"Well, you mop up the floor and you can have breakfast."

Wesley took the mop. "Sure thing I know how to use this." He went to the bathroom, mopped the floor and returned.

"Here, I'll take the mop," said Mattie. "Sit down over there."

"Yeow, that sure smells good." Wesley sat at the table.

"Hand me your plate. I guess you want everything but the tomatoes."

"I like everything but tomatoes. I can't stand tomatoes."

Mattie took Wesley's plate to the stove and dumped on scrambled eggs. "You ever had fried green tomatoes?"

"No." Wesley chugged his orange juice.

"Oh, my Lord, I forgot the biscuits." She opened the oven, reached in, got the pan of biscuits, dropped it on the stove top, picked it up and dropped it again so the biscuits would break away from the pan bottom. "Well, they're not too bad. You like yours brown anyway, don't you?"

"Yeah."

"Well, there you go." Mattie handed Wesley his plate— four slices of bacon, eggs, grits, two biscuits, and three slices of cold cantaloupe, then another glass of orange juice.

Wesley grabbed a biscuit and took a bite.

"Wait a minute, until we say the blessing." He didn't

know any better, Mattie thought to herself. "Do you want to say the blessing?"

"No."

Mattie stood by the table. "Dear Lord, we are grateful for these and all the many blessings made possible through Thy bountiful love. In Thy precious name. Amen." She picked up her plate off the table and returned to the stove. "Did you ever stick your finger in a biscuit?"

Wesley looked up and froze. What the hell? "Do what?"

"Stick your finger in your biscuit." Mattie sat at the table. "Like this." She held her biscuit and stuck her finger in so that it passed from one end, the long way—inside the biscuit—almost to the other end, stopping short of breaking through. She pulled her finger back out. "Then pour in molasses. Like this." She slowly poured in molasses, then took a bite. "It's good. Try it. Or you can use your knife handle."

"Wait a minute." Wesley tood a bite of eggs, a bite of grits, and two bites of bacon. While he chewed he stuck his finger in a biscuit, pulled it out, poured in molasses, and took a big bite. Molasses rolled out over his hand. "That's pretty neat," he said, his mouth full, looking at the biscuit, almost half gone. He licked molasses off his hand. "What do you make these biscuits out of?"

"Buttermilk, Crisco, and flour. Easy. You want some coffee?"

"No." Wesley mopped molasses off his plate with a biscuit. "Can I have some more orange juice?"

Mattie got up and got the orange juice from the refrigerator and poured his glass full. "There you go." He could say something about the food, she thought. "How's the food?"

"Good. Real good."

"You have some trouble with your teeth, don't you?"

"My *teeth*?"

"Yeah. Don't you have teeth trouble."

"Yeah. But what the hell?"

Mattie put the carton of orange juice back in the refrigerator. "Well, the reason I asked is I might be able to help you get them fixed up. I know it's expensive and all, but if you'll go to a dentist and find out what it'll cost, I'll see if I can't help you out maybe. They can do all kinds of things these days to make your teeth look better. And they are one of your most important assets. Don't you think?"

"Yeah, I guess. I never thought about it. Except when I got a toothache."

"Did your mama or daddy or the orphanage or anybody ever take you to the dentist?"

"Hell, no." She knew about the damn orphanage, thought Wesley. She *is* my grandma. She just don't want to say so yet.

"Teeth make such a big difference, and you don't realize it until they start giving you trouble."

"I been realizing stuff all my life."

"Well, I've worked real hard all my life to keep mine up. You just didn't have as good a start as I did."

"I need a pickup more'n I need good teeth."

"Oh no you don't."

"I get me a pickup and I can earn a living and be fixing up my teeth for the rest of my life."

"You need to get started out on a solid footing with good teeth. It'll influence everything that happens from now on."

Wesley cleaned his plate with the remains of his biscuit. He reached for another biscuit. "I think I'll just have one more of these with some molasses."

He has a direct way about him, like Lamar, thought Mattie. It's like some good is in there somewhere—and just needs a chance to grow, spread out until it covers a little more of him. "You want me to cut your hair?"

"Yeah. Yeah, I sure do."

He probably hadn't ever said "ma'am" in his life. "Well, take your plate over to the sink when you're finished. Let me get the clippers and I'll do you sitting right there."

Mattie got a bed sheet from the bedroom closet.

Wesley took his plate to the sink and then sat back down. Hell, if I get new teeth, a haircut, some of them mirror sunglasses, won't nobody in the world know me. Hell, *I* won't even know me.

"I can take another bath and wash the hair out," said Wesley.

"Not this morning."

"Why not?"

"You can't take another bath here until you learn the rules."

"What rules?"

"Bathroom rules: just a little bit of water and you clean up after yourself. Let's see," said Mattie, safety-pinning the sheet at the back of Wesley's neck. "I'll vacuum your head when I finish cutting."

"*Vacuum?*"

"Yes."

After Mattie cut with scissors, she used the electric barber clippers that Paul had bought when he went to barber school. After barber school he began working at the cigarette factory. Then he bought the Listre Hardware from Alvin Terrill and spent forty years running it, always sitting at home in the mornings, reading the paper, not talking to anybody unless it was to tell them to be quiet or to bring him something. Sometimes Mattie wondered if Paul had really had to be that way. And then he often got home late at night after she'd finished helping the kids with their homework.

"Here, let me put the clippers to these little tufts of hair on your face."

"Leave the mustache."

"Oh, I didn't see it."

Mattie cut the sprouts of hair with the electric clippers. Wesley followed the clippers with his eyes, holding his head very still.

Mattie had helped Robert and Elaine with their homework until they were so far along she didn't know what they were doing, had no idea of what the questions and problems meant even after she'd read the assignment herself. This boy probably never got that far. She remembered leaving their books and confusing questions, and looking through their closets to find something that needed sewing, a missing button, a hem, a pocket, and while they fretted with the homework, she would sew their clothes.

And she wondered if any of that could somehow ex-

plain why they never got married, leaving her no grandchildren to care for, no grandchildren to accompany her
into the black future, grandchildren with the blood of
her uncles Fred, Hudson, and Smiley, her aunts Thelma,
Lola, Terry, Okie, Bobbie, Chloe, her mother, her father.
If her mother could only have lived for Elaine and Robert
to meet and talk to. *She* could have somehow shown
them, convinced them that having a family was more
important than anything in the world, more important
than anything on earth. Did that make sense? It did
make sense. If it were between Elaine living with no
children and dying while having one who lived—that
would be a tough choice—if that baby were to be the
family's only survivor. Well, of course she'd pick Elaine.
She shouldn't even think about that, but then again
maybe she should think about it. After all, through the
blood is the only way you really can give of your *true*
self—the self that is in your blood and that has been
there since Adam, that stream of blood flowing unbroken
since Adam and Eve, winding through those brambles
and ditches and deserts and jungles and wars and fam-
ines—in her family's case, to now end with the death of
the children of Mattie Rigsbee. There must be some
other way to think about it, Mattie thought. Here's a
young man I can do something for, if not in blood, in
spirit. Jesus talked about the spirit too.

Mattie got the hand mirror and handed it to Wesley.
"How does that look?"

"A little whopsided."

"How so?"

"This side is shorter."

"Well, I ain't got a whole lot of time. Let's see. It is a little whopsided. Let me just trim this a little more." She trimmed and combed. "There now. That okay?"

"Yeah, I guess."

Mattie rolled the vacuum cleaner from the closet into the kitchen, attached the duster and vacuumed Wesley's head.

While driving to church, Mattie asked Wesley if he wanted to go to Sunday school in the Young People's Department or if he wanted to stay with her. He said he'd stay with her.

She would quietly escort Wesley through Sunday school and church, the warm experience of it, before he was off to see his friend and if any of it rubbed off on him, if church and any of its goodness rubbed off on him, then he and his friend would be the better for it. That was all she could do.

With the haircut and Robert's shirt and tie, she'd gotten him in pretty good shape. He looked all right, except for his teeth.

Wesley sat with Mattie during the assembly program, then walked with her into her Sunday school class. He was wearing Robert's light blue shirt with the white collar and navy blue tie with little red lions.

In the classroom Mattie stopped in front of a chair. Wesley, lagging slightly behind—looking for, seeing a pocketbook that was open, wondering how to get over there to sit close to it—bumped into her. Mattie spoke to the group of seven women, all of whom were looking at

Wesley. "You-all, this is Wesley Benfield. Wesley, this is my Sunday school class."

Wesley nodded and frowned.

The women eyed Wesley pleasantly—smiled and nodded, except for Beatrice, who stared. That name: Wesley Benfield. Where had she . . . ?—that short article in the morning paper. She spoke loudly: "A Wesley Benfield escaped from the YMRC Friday night. It was in the paper this morning—a little article. He was about sixteen, too. They caught another one trying the same thing."

"Won't me."

He told me he was on leave, Mattie thought.

"I was thinking this morning if it was any of the Benfields I used to teach," said Beatrice. "And this one's name was Wesley, too. Just like you. And about your age."

Wesley glared at her. "Well, it won't me." That awful woman staring at him, big earrings, thick powder on her face. He stared back as long as he could, then looked at Mattie.

Mattie was horribly confused. As she sat, she said, "Well, he's not the same one. This is my cousin's boy."

"Beatrice, Mattie wouldn't bring an escaped convict to Sunday school," someone said, and laughed.

"I'm from Arizona," said Wesley. He sat beside Mattie and picked up a hymnbook. That woman was liable to call the law, and they were liable to come surround the place. If they did he'd . . . he'd . . . just put on one of them choir dresses and sing in the choir and they'd never know he was there. He'd hide right in the middle of them. That would be awesome—the last place on earth they'd look for him. Hell, he could do that anyway. Then he could sneak out amongst the crowd, borrow a car from the parking lot and haul ass. That would be the safest way to do it and—what a genius move.

"Let's bow for the opening prayer," said the lady at the wood thing up front.

Mattie prayed silently. Dear God, I didn't know. Peter lied too. I didn't have no idea . . .

Wesley looked around. There was a bulletin board display on the wall at the front of the class. An angel with an extended hand stood behind a church. From her hand orange strings extended to groups of people of different colors from different nations. The title of the display was "Missions." There was a chalkboard along one wall, and a flip chart of maps by the door.

". . . and be with the sick and afflicted in the hospital beds throughout this nation, throughout this state, this county. We especially ask Thy blessing upon those members of our church who are now sick, especially Trixie Byrd, and the Collingwood boy. And now be with us as we study Thy word. We are especially grateful for our visitor this morning. Please bless him in this hour. All things in Thy blessed name. Amen."

I, I need to think, thought Mattie. I'll tell them he needed Sunday school and church. I had to lie—Peter had to lie. Mine was a little white lie because this boy needed church so bad. Now maybe after church I can make him go back like he's supposed to. Maybe he'll let me take him back.

"Okay, let's open our quarterlies to today's lesson," said Carrie. "The scripture is from Psalms."

Mattie had not read her lesson. She was astonished at herself. She had never once come to Sunday school unprepared. Was the Devil behind this: the whole thing. Should she just get up this minute and go make a phone call to the YMRC? Go get a newspaper? Or should she . . . Dear gentle Jesus, guide and direct me in this hour of need. Help me to understand what Thou wouldst have me do.

Mattie relaxed her shoulders and looked at Wesley. He was reading from the hymnbook. She put her finger on the scripture passage in her Bible, slipped toward him and held the Bible between them so he could look on. This was not working out right at all.

"The earth is the Lord's, and the fullness thereof; the world, and they that dwell therein . . ."

Wesley held the hymnbook as he looked at the Bible. Mattie pushed the Bible closer to him so he would hold it with her. He put the hymnbook in the empty chair beside him, and held to the Bible. Mattie placed her finger on the passage.

Carrie taught the lesson from the quarterly. She said that the Psalmist was talking about how the earth is the Lord's and that one day he's coming back to claim it no matter what; that we should remember that America may be providing what amounts to the world's last hope.

As the lesson continued, Beatrice fidgeted with her handkerchief more and more. She was going to *have* to do something. Call the authorities. Mattie must have made some mistake; she was getting quite old. That boy could be dangerous.

Mattie tried to think—to untangle the confusion in

her head. What should she do? Wesley must have escaped. But he needed the church—all the more now.

Wesley thumbed through the hymnal, came across "Shall We Gather at the River" and studied the words: ". . . where bright angel feet have trod." Muddy bright angel feet on the riverbank, he thought. Bright lights between their toes, shining through the mud. That one's feet on the bulletin board was behind the church. Bright angel feet jumping all around in the grass. White bright feet with neon blue blood vessels. He'd like to marry somebody with bright angel feet.

When the lesson was over, they all stood for the final song. Wesley picked up the hymnbook and fumbled to find the right page. The head woman played the piano and they all started singing: "This is my Father's world, and to my listening ears . . ."

Carrie gave the closing prayer, and dismissed them. Several women remained. Hanna Brown talked to Wesley: "We hadn't had a young man in here since I don't know when. It freshens up the place."

"That's because I had a good bath last night."

I've got to talk to him, thought Mattie.

"What?" Hanna leaned toward Wesley, smiling, with a frown around her eyes.

"That's because I had a good bath last night. I wouldn't have freshened up the place before then." Wesley looked around for the woman who'd put the finger on him. He didn't see her. He was going to have to do something, leave or hide, one.

Hanna laughed. "Did you hear that Mattie. He said he had a good bath last night."

"He did have a good bath last night."

"He's such a funny young man."

Beatrice was on the phone in the church office. "He's with Mrs. Mattie Rigsbee, Paul Rigsbee's wife. She won't be sitting with Paul—he's dead. She'll probably be sitting with Carrie Bowers about halfway down on the left. Carrie's wearing a white hat. . . . That's right. . . . Yes . . . Mattie's a widow. Paul died of a heart attack five or six, let's see, five years ago. Went in the blinking of a eye sitting in his car at the stoplight on Tuney Lake Road. Thank goodness he won't driving along. . . . Yes, okay, you're welcome."

Only Mattie and Wesley remained in the Sunday school classroom.

"Sit down," said Mattie.

They both sat down.

"Did you escape?" said Mattie, looking straight ahead.

"Well, I sort of did." Wesley looked out the window, at the bulletin board with the "Missions" display, at the announcement written in yellow chalk on the chalkboard: "Bus leaves for White Lake Saturday at 9AM. Sign up in the office."

Sheriff Walter Tillman and Deputy Larry Hollins, of Hanson County, on car patrol, received radio orders from headquarters. They drove toward the church. "I'll go in the front door after they get started," said the sheriff, "and that'll be in the back of everybody. You get somewhere behind the preacher, somewhere you can see from—maybe there's a door—so you can see him and catch him if he tries to run out that way. I'll wait outside the front door. When you get positioned, give me two clicks on the walkie-talkie; I'll come in and when I spot him I'll arrest him."

"And you told me you were on leave," said Mattie, looking at Wesley. "Well, well. This is some fix."

"I think maybe I better get out of here," said Wesley, standing, glancing at Mattie. "Now I'm a wanted man. I'm headed south for Florida."

"You ain't growed up enough to be a wanted man. That's one of your problems. I wanted you to spend one Sunday morning in church . . . in a good church. You should have done your time. You shouldn't have escaped. It'll make it that much worse when they catch you. What are you going to use for transportation?"

"Them." Wesley pointed to his feet.

"Well, if you ain't out of town by 12:30 or 1:00 then stop by for dinner. I got all that food, and it's ready. You might as well." Lord have mercy, I've lied once, thought Mattie. Peter did it three times. I might as well feed him before he leaves.

Wesley stood. "Well, I'm getting out of here. See you later. If anybody wants to know where I am just say south of the border. Say he said he was going south of the border." He walked out.

Now there's that extra pork chop, thought Mattie. Well, well. If they catch him, I hope they catch him gently. She stood to go upstairs to the sanctuary for church service.

Wesley moved along a hall toward a door which led outside. Two children were just inside the door, two women just outside. The women were holding black pocketbooks. He could sure use a pocketbook or two. He pushed open the door and stepped outside. He wouldn't hide in the choir—if the coast was clear, he'd borrow a car. Suddenly there was a sheriff's patrol car coming down the road toward him; he spun around, walked back inside, stopped and watched the car slow, stop. Two uniformed lawmen got out, hitched their belts, and looked around. Wesley saw stairs at the far end of the hall. He'd better walk slowly, carefully. He'd go upstairs, find a closet or something. Mrs. Rigsbee would tell them he'd gone, left, and somewhere up there in a closet or something would be the safest place in the world. He could stay until everybody was gone. The choir would be too risky. He could *say* that's what he did. He walked up the stairs, holding himself to one step at a time. He wanted to sprint. He reached the top of the stairs and turned the corner. Damn. Choir members, in long dress things, were filing through a door. Jesus. That Beatrice woman was one of them. He'd have to go back downstairs and hide in a room down there. He turned and started back down the stairs. Feet. Coming up. Black spit-shined shoes, pants with a stripe. *The Law.* He turned on the stairs. He'd have to walk past the choir people. No, the last one was going through the door.

He hurried into the room the choir had left; there was a long, open closet—dress things inside. He heard footsteps. The footsteps stopped, then shuffled. The choir and congregation started singing. His heart knocked rapidly in his head and throat. He pulled a dress off a hanger, put it on, zipped it, picked up a hymnbook. He would go with the choir plan—hide in plain sight. He started for the choir door. In the hallway he met the deputy: shiny badge, all that leather, and a big pistol up under the elbow. The deputy spoke: "Can I see the whole auditorium in there from that door you think?" he asked, his hat in his hand, motioning toward the entrance to the choir.

"I don't know. Yeah. Yeah, I think so."

"There's a boy in there we need. Escaped from the RC. I gotta be able to see the place from back here."

"Un huh, okay."

Wesley stepped up the steps and into the doorway leading into where the choir was standing, singing. They were loud: "Ye chosen seed of Israel's race . . ." He held onto the door frame, licked sweat from his upper lip. There were several seats at the near end of the last row there in front of him.

The deputy stepped on Wesley's heel, leaned against him. "Excuse me."

Wesley smelled the deputy's aftershave. He stepped in. The voices of the congregation singing hit him full force.

Mattie, from her pew, noticed one of the choir members coming in late.

Deputy Hollins, trying to stay concealed, yet see from the door to the choir, suddenly realized that the way he could be the least conspicuous would be to get a robe and get in the choir, there on the back row. Otherwise, the suspect might see him peeping in the door. He found a robe in the choir room, and as he moved into the choir, he signaled Sheriff Tillman with two clicks on his walkie-talkie.

The sheriff had been waiting at the top of the steps just outside the closed front door of the church—wondering what the dickens was taking Hollins so long. When he heard the two clicks of static on his walkie-talkie, he stepped inside.

Dodson Clark, an usher, stood just inside the door, cleaning his fingernails with his new Swiss Army knife. Dodson, when he was growing up, aspired to be two things in life, a fireman and a church usher, the former so that he could live dangerously, the latter so that he could stand or sit in the foyer during the entire church service—sliding out into a back room or even outside at will.

Dodson looked up to see the sheriff. "Well, hey, Sheriff," he said, above the sound of the music. "You are Sheriff Tillman, ain't you?"

"That's right. How you doing?" said the sheriff, taking off his hat.

"Welcome to Listre Baptist. Here," Dodson picked up a church-service bulletin."

"Oh no. I'm trying to pick up a young man might be with a Mrs. Mattie Rigsbee, who supposed to be sitting—"

"She's about halfway down on the—"

"About halfway down on the left."

"Let's move right over here and we can see; yeah, there she is, beside Carrie Bowers with—"

"A white hat."

"—a white hat. Yeah." Dodson looked at the sheriff.

"No boy there. There's supposed to be a male with her: Caucasian, sixteen years of age, five feet nine, sandy hair, light complexion."

Dodson pictured a sixteen-year-old youth—he'd better be Caucasian—standing and spraying the congregation with machine-gun fire. Dodson would duck, crawl along under the pews, grab the assailant by the ankles, pull hard, trip him up, disarm him.

"How about going down and getting her," said the sheriff to Dodson, "and asking her to come back here so we can step outside and I can ask her a few questions."

Dodson asked young Terry Miles, another usher, if he'd mind going down and getting Mrs. Rigsbee. He, Dodson, needed to stay with the sheriff.

Alora and Hanna Brown stood together, singing the opening song, three rows behind Mattie and Carrie. Finner was in a small room upstairs, taping the service for shut-ins. Alora had noticed a young man, then an older man, both strangers, slip into the choir. Then she saw Terry Miles come down, get Mattie and lead her out. As the song ended, Mattie came back to her seat.

The sheriff, standing outside the front door, clicked his walkie-talkie button three times, the signal for "meet me at the vehicle." He'd learned from Mrs. Rigsbee that the Benfield boy had fled the scene.

"Who is them strangers in the choir?" Alora whispered to Hanna, as Clarence Vernon made the morning announcements—just after the opening song.

"Where?"

"On the back row. There, that one slipping out, and the other one, standing beside Bill Parker."

"Oh, I believe that's the young man was in Sunday school. He had a fresh bath last night he said. Maybe he's going to sing a solo."

Alora whispered, "What was he doing in your Sunday school?"

"He was with Mattie. Look, he's leaving, too," whispered Hanna.

After the service, Harvey Odum stood in the almost empty church parking lot. He was talking to his wife, who stood beside him, frowning, rubbing her bare arm as if she were cold. He put his hand behind his head and looked around. "I *know* I parked it here," he said.

X

Soon after the church service, Mattie, in the kitchen, looked into her oven. The biscuits were about ready. Robert and Laurie, Robert's new girlfriend, sat at the table, sipping iced tea, ready to eat.

A maroon Chrysler LeBaron eased up to the back door, on the lawn, well out of sight of the road out front.

"Who is that?" Robert asked Mattie.

"I don't know."

"Why did they pull up on the lawn like that?" asked Laurie. Laurie had practically no chin and curly black hair.

Robert was worried. His mother was hardly talking, even though Laurie was asking questions, like Laurie seemed to do quite a bit. That was one of the things Robert liked about Laurie. She knew how to bring people out. But what worried him was that his mother was one of the last persons on earth who he'd thought would ever need bringing out, yet here she was being brought out by Laurie. His mother was too quiet today.

Whoever that was, thought Mattie, would be bringing news or questions about what happened at church. "I was going to tell you what happened at church today," said Mattie to Robert. She needed to explain—the truth—so it wouldn't seem like she was some kind of criminal. And now here was no telling who, and she hadn't had a chance to explain to Robert yet. This young woman kept asking all these questions.

Mattie walked to the back door to meet whoever it was. She saw Alora and Finner walking over from their house. Who could— *Wesley*!

"I come to eat."

"Well, come on in. It's on the table. Who's . . . ? Did you . . . ? Alora, y'all come on in."

Robert looked at the young man coming in the back door. Something about his clothes looked familiar. Very familiar. Indeed, this fellow was wearing Robert's own light blue shirt with the white collar and his navy blue tie with the little red lions on it.

"Y'all, this is Wesley. Wesley Benfield," Mattie said to Robert and Laurie. "This is my son Robert, and Laurie Thomas, his friend," said Mattie. "And let's see, this is Alora and Finner Swanson."

"Is that my tie?" asked Robert.

"Yeah, your shirt, too." Wesley nodded toward Mattie, "Grandma said I could wear them."

"*Grandma*?"

"Could be. Can't ever tell, you know." I ain't no kin to *you*, though, thought Wesley.

The sheriff's patrol car pulled up in the backyard behind the maroon Chrysler.

"Y'all are all kin?" Laurie asked Robert. This is strange, she thought.

"Go ahead and get you something to eat," said Mattie to Wesley. "There on the stove. There's a plate. We were about to start. Alora, don't y'all want something?"

"No, we ain't kin," said Robert.

"Naw," said Alora, "we already eat. We just wanted to find out what was going on in church this morning. What all that mix-up was about."

"Ain't that Harvey Odum's LeBaron?" said Finner.

Mattie looked at Wesley.

"I ain't sure what his name is," said Wesley. "I borrowed it." Wesley had a plate and was spooning on creamed potatoes. He forked a pork chop onto his plate. "I'm going to take it by his house." He made a little indentation in the top of his potatoes and spooned on thick gravy. He looked out the back window. There was the sheriff peering through the window of the LeBaron. Wesley took a bite of potatoes, put his plate down on the stove. "I got to go to the bathroom." He turned and walked through the kitchen and den and to the front door where he held on to the knob and looked through one of the small squares of glass. A deputy was leaning against another patrol

car on the side of the road. He walked down the hall
and into Mattie's room and looked out into the backyard.
The sheriff was at the back door and the deputy who
had stood right beside him in the choir was leaning
against the sheriff's car. Hot waves spread from Wesley's scalp down over his neck and shoulders. They had
the front, back, and both sides covered. He walked
across the hall into his and Robert's bedroom, closed the
door, opened the dresser and got out the pajamas he'd
worn the night before. This was it. They had him. He'd
get in bed and tell them he was too sick to move. Heart
trouble.

Mattie stood at the back-door screen. "Come on in,
Sheriff," she said.

"Mrs. Rigsbee, this car has been reported as stolen. Is
Wesley Benfield here?"

"Yes, but I wadn't expecting him. Come on in. Maybe
you'd like a little bite to eat."

"A stolen car?" said Alora. "Mattie?"

"We been on this wild goose chase all morning," said
the sheriff, stepping inside, "as you know."

"He went back there," said Robert to the sheriff. "He's
got on my shirt and tie."

"You never met him before?" Laurie asked Robert.

"He might have left out the front. I don't know," said
Mattie.

"No, I never met him," said Robert.

"We got the front covered," said the sheriff. "And the
back and both sides."

"What did he do?" Laurie asked the sheriff.

"Auto theft," said the sheriff. "Escape from the RC. That's the most recent thing anyway. He's not armed as anyone knows, is he?"

"Oh no," said Mattie, who was moving toward the food on the counter and taking up a serving dish, "he ain't armed. You-all sit down. I'll get him. Have you had dinner, Sheriff?"

"No ma'am, but—"

"Get you a plate up there. Robert, get him a plate. You got time to eat a bite. Wesley needs to eat a bite before he goes with y'all. I'll get him. I got a bowl of beef stew I can warm up in no time at all."

Mattie walked to the front door and opened it. "Wesley didn't come out here, did he?" she asked the deputy.

"No ma'am. Ain't he in there?"

"I think he might be in the bathroom. Don't you want a bite to eat? You must be hungry; it's almost one o'clock."

"I'm supposed to stay out here."

Mattie walked down the hall to check the bathroom. The door was open. He wasn't in there. She opened the door to the bedroom. There he was, in bed, covered up, face down, the pillow over his head. He was crying. Mattie closed the door behind her, sat down on the other single bed. "Son, come on and finish your dinner. It'll be all right."

Wesley said into the bed: "I'm not going back to the goddamned RC."

"Son, I've asked you not to cuss in this house."

Wesley removed the pillow, rolled over on his back. His face was splotched red and white. "I just wanted something to eat."

"You come on. You can get something to eat."

Mattie looked out the window. A highway patrol car was pulling up.

Wesley raised up on his elbow and looked out the window.

The sheriff knocked on the bedroom door. "Mrs. Rigsbee? Is the suspect in there?"

"Yes. He'll be out in a minute."

The door opened. Robert stood behind the sheriff.

"He's right here," said Mattie. "Now, if you-all will wait a minute we'll be right out to finish eating. Then you can go."

"Mrs. Rigsbee, I need to arrest this man."

"Well, just tell him he's arrested."

"You're under arrest." The sheriff took a step forward, and hitched up his belt.

"Now, go back to the kitchen and get some food on your plate. We'll be right out. He's just a boy."

"Boy, my foot, Mama," said Robert.

"Robert, go sit down at the table and start eating."

"I'm sick," said Wesley to the sheriff. "I got heart trouble and if you move me from here I can sue you for malpractice."

"Malpractice?" said the sheriff to himself, squinting his eyes and showing his teeth slightly. "Malpractice? Son, I ought to put you in jail for being silly. Get dressed and let's go."

"We'll be right out," said Mattie. "You've got my word."

"Don't you try anything," said the sheriff to Wesley. He and Robert went back to the kitchen.

"They got me," said Wesley.

"Yes, they do. Get up now and put your clothes on."

Wesley uncovered himself, swung his legs over the side of the bed and sat up. He looked over his shoulder out the window and saw the sheriff's car and the highway patrol car. He slowly toppled onto his side on the bed.

"You got to go, son," said Mattie.

"Are you my grandma? Lamar said you won't."

"I don't know." Mattie searched for a way, an excuse, a reason to say yes. This boy was in need and, well, he deserved a grandma, everybody did, and she might as well be it. It had been an unusual day. "Maybe I am."

"I thought so." He sat up. "Well, could I come live here? If I had a place to live they might let me out. They were going to one time."

"Son, I'm slowing down. I can't just up and keep somebody here."

Wesley fell back onto his side.

"Mattie?" Alora stuck her head in the door. "They sent me back here to get y'all."

"Alora, get back in the kitchen; we'll be right out."

"Well," said Wesley, lying on the bed, his feet hanging over the side. "I'm going to kill myself then."

Alora heard, rushed back up the hall to the kitchen. "He's fixing to commit sideways!" she said.

"What?" said the sheriff.

"Commit sideways—kill hisself."

"You mean suicide?" said Laurie.

"Right. Whatever."

"He's *armed*?" asked the sheriff.

"Good gracious," said Finner. "I'll go get my gun."

"No." The sheriff held out his hand, as if stopping traffic. "Don't go get your gun. I knew I should have got him," said the sheriff. He started down the hall to the bedroom. He met Mattie. "Where is he?"

"He's fixing to take a bath."

"Oh, no. We got to get him out of here." The sheriff heard water running in the tub. He stepped to the closed bathroom door, opened it, and faced the back of a naked boy.

Wesley was pouring shampoo into the water.

"Let's go, son." He don't look like he's about to kill hisself, thought the sheriff—all them suds.

"I just want to take a bath." Wesley looked over his shoulder. "I should be allowed one bath. Look, look at them suds. Just one bath, man. One little bath. I'll be five minutes."

"No way; let's go. I'm gonna wait for you to eat. That's all I can do for you. You better be happy for that."

"Look at them suds."

"I know. Let's go now. Don't make me handcuff you."

"Shit." Wesley turned off the water, stepped into his pajama bottoms, walked past the sheriff, standing in the bathroom door, and into the bedroom. He dressed in his jeans, loafers, and navy blue T-shirt with a pocket. This was it. It was all over. They had him.

The sheriff watched Wesley dress, then followed him to the kitchen.

Mattie was getting the potatoes from the stove. Robert, Laurie, and Wesley sat at the dinner table. The sheriff called the choir deputy, Larry Hollins, inside and told the other deputy and the highway patrolman they could leave. Larry positioned himself in the kitchen near the back porch door. As he passed the dinner table, he looked at Wesley twice. There was something familiar . . . Wesley's back was to him as he stood by the back porch door.

The sheriff stood in the den, where Alora and Finner sat.

"You sure you-all don't want something to eat?" asked Mattie, setting the pot of creamed potatoes on the table.

"No thanks," said the sheriff. "We just got a cheeseburger at Hardee's."

"The chicken filet at Hardee's is good," said Alora. "More meat."

"Now, let's see," said Laurie to Mattie, "where did you and Wesley meet?" I wonder if I can get all this straight, she thought.

"At the RC."

"My Sunday school class visited out there one time," said Laurie. "It's an interesting place, isn't it?"

"Yes. Yes, it is," said Mattie, standing at the stove. "Let's say the blessing so we can eat."

"I said it once," said Robert.

"Well, I'm going to say it again. Lord bless this food to the nourishment . . ."

Wesley looked around over his shoulder. The choir deputy was staring at him.

". . . we pray in Thy blessed name. Amen."

Robert, Laurie, and Wesley started passing food. Peas and corn, creamed potatoes, pork chops, a pickle plate, string beans, sliced tomatoes, biscuits. Robert would not hand food directly to Wesley but instead set it on the table for Wesley to pick up. On the stove was beef stew, turnip salet, potato salad, and cornbread. "Let me have your plates," said Mattie. "I'll get you a little of this over here on the stove."

In the den, Finner stood up, bent over and turned on the television. "Let's see if the ball game is on."

"Who's playing?" asked the sheriff.

"Braves."

"Did you see that game last week?"

"Yeah. Good one, won't it?"

"Sure was."

With a pot holder, Mattie picked up the frying pan holding the cornbread and held it in front of Larry, the deputy, still standing by the back door. "Don't you at least want a piece of this cornbread?"

"Well, I reckon I can take a little piece."

"It sure is good," said Laurie.

The sheriff is watching television, thought Wesley. If she'd hit the deputy in the head with that frying pan, then I could . . . No, she wouldn't do it. It's over. I'm back in. But she didn't tell the deputy or anybody in church. She seen me in the choir. She was on my side. Pulling for me through the whole thing. She's got to be my grandma. If I could get some kind of letter of proof or something, I could live here. Then I could even maybe do something to get some of them medals. Get in some clubs; go back to high school. Hell, I could even go back to high school— if I could live here and do it.

"Don't you want a little bite to eat?" Mattie asked Larry. "There's plenty of room for you to sit down."

"I reckon I could eat a little bit," said Larry. "All right if I eat a bite, Sheriff?" he asked.

The sheriff, sitting on the edge of a footstool watching the game, looked up. "What?"

"Okay if I sit down for a bite to eat."

"Yeah. Watch the prisoner. You had a cheeseburger."

"I know it, but it just was a little one."

Larry sat down beside Wesley and stared at him. "Won't you in the choir this morning? Was that . . . ?"

"Was that you up there?" Mattie asked Larry. "Came in late? It was too far for me to see. Here, have a pork chop."

"Yeah, I was up there. We were planning to apprehend the suspect there in the church. But he was already . . ." Larry looked at Wesley again. "I swear the guy went in right before me looked exactly like you."

"Could I have another piece of cornbread?" Wesley asked Mattie.

Mattie stood to get the cornbread.

"He can get it," said Robert.

"I can get it."

"So you two know each other," said Laurie, looking first at Larry, then at Wesley. This is just so unusual, she thought.

"No, we don't," said Larry. "I just—"

"To tell the truth," said Wesley. "That was me. That was really me. I can just about be anywhere I want to at anytime I want to. I'm just that way." He took a bite of cornbread. "I like the dangerous life. I court excitement."

"Well, I declare," said Mattie. "I saw two men come in late, but I couldn't make out who they were. I told the sheriff you were *gone*."

"Did you sing anything?" Laurie asked Larry.

"Naw. I got signaled from the sheriff to meet him at the car."

"Then I left," said Wesley, "after he left. You didn't know that first song either, did you?"

"I don't remember." Larry looked at the sheriff watching the ball game in the dining room, then said in a low voice, "Would y'all do me a favor and don't mention to the sheriff about us both being up there in the choir at the same time? I can't believe that."

"Don't worry about it, man," said Wesley. "It's part of my nature to outfox the law."

"You must have had an interesting life," said Laurie to Wesley.

"Yeah. I have."

"What's it like at the RC?"

"Pretty weird." Wesley remembered the dining room at the RC. Plain green plastered walls. Plastic dishes, bland foods. He'd be there tonight with Ted, Mex, Terry, Blake. He'd tell them he'd been in Las Vegas; he'd caught a plane, won fifty, no, eighty thousand dollars and then lost it all, but not before buying a Trans Am and cruising the town with two women who'd followed him around until he'd asked them what they wanted and they'd told him they wanted him, that they'd seen him in the movies they thought; they went to a motel and he made it with both of them; then the law got after him and there was a nine-hour chase across Nevada until they finally caught him after a car crash and a long foot chase—finally put a German shepherd on him and he'd had to take his jacket off and wrap it around his arm and stick it in the dog's mouth.

Robert was thinking about the symptoms. What condition was his mother entering? Was it a phase of some sort? Was she having some of those tiny strokes they talk about? Or Alzheimer's? What would they say about all this at the church? Wesley was singing in the choir for some reason? And his mother watching him? And the sheriff? It sounded like her reputation could be in some danger. Maybe she needed a long rest. She was slowing down. She was right about that. But she wouldn't let you do anything. And how did she manage to get to know this young . . . young . . . thief. Of all people. He was one—or just like one—of those guys who traveled around in a pickup truck asking old people if they'd like their roof fixed for three hundred dollars, in advance. That's the type he was, all right. And his own mother had bought it all—which supported the small-stroke theory because it was not like her to be taken in by anything— or to take in anything: not a dog, not a cat, much less a character like this. "Could I have my tie back, please?" Robert asked Wesley.

"What?" Wesley's fork-stuck cucumber slice stopped halfway to his mouth.

"My tie. Could I have it back now?"

Mattie spoke: "He might need it at the RC, son."

"He might need it? It's *my* tie. *I* might need it."

"Do you have a tie at the RC?" Mattie asked Wesley.

"Nope."

"You might need it for a church service. Don't they have church services?"

"Something like that," said Wesley chewing.

"Well, you could wear it then."

"But it's *my tie*," said Robert.

"You've got at least twenty ties, Robert."

"Why don't you just adopt him?"

"Robert!"

"He's wearing my clothes! I could press charges. There's the sheriff right there."

"Son, he's never had what you've had." Mattie stood to organize the desserts.

"No, no, he hasn't, but he's slowly getting it."

"You won't miss those clothes, Robert."

"I already miss them."

"I'll buy you a new shirt and tie." Mattie looked up from the desserts. "I got apple pie, ice cream, and pound cake for dessert. Who wants what?"

"I'll take a little of all three," said Wesley, eyeing the hot apple pie.

Robert asked for pound cake. Well, he thought, the little jerk would be put away in an hour or two, and sometime during the next day or two he could have a heart-to-heart talk with his mother. It had been a long time since they'd had one, anyway. She would always talk heart-to-heart to him, about some Sunday school lesson, Billy Graham, or something in the Bible. But this time he'd ask her if she'd been feeling funny. He'd better call Elaine and tell her what all was going on. She might be able to do something. If there were some agency that could help out, Elaine'd know about it. If worse came to worst he could move in with his mother—sell the condo. And maybe she'd slow down so much that their conversations could even out a bit—she'd slow down enough to listen for a while.

Mattie asked Finner, Alora, and the sheriff if they wanted some dessert. They all said yes, came to get it, and took it back to the den. Alora almost sat down at the dinner table, but she was worried that the prisoner might take her hostage. You don't have to be young to get raped these days, she reminded herself. You'd think after you got a little husky, and older, they wouldn't rape you, but they would. Didn't a day pass but you read about it in the newspaper: some woman, raped. She picked up her purse off the floor and put it in her lap. Anything could happen right here. That boy might jump that deputy, steal his gun, and there might be a gunfight. Somebody could be shot dead, and if a gunfight did start she would pull out her new .22. Nobody knew she had it. She'd shoot that boy right in the head. He'd be aiming at the sheriff. They'd put her picture in the paper. If she didn't shoot him, he'd probably rape her. He might take her hostage and drive her all over the United States and do no telling what to her. And even if she got to see the Grand Canyon it wouldn't be worth it. It would be humiliating. She would just die. And even if he did take her hostage he would never suspect that she had a gun in her purse and as soon as he wasn't looking she could pull it out and shoot him. They'd put her picture in the paper and she'd let them go ahead and do one of those tests to show that she *had not* been raped so that they could print that information along with her picture, to dispel rumors. Sometimes you could never be quite sure about some of those younger women that got raped. You always wondered a tiny little bit.

Mattie asked if anybody wanted a second helping of dessert. She wanted everybody to be full and satisfied. This had been the most unusual day—strange, full, brimming, yet sad—and had just about worn her out with all the strange bright sparkles and dark fogs. She couldn't keep up with all that had happened. She had hoped Wesley could be touched by his visit to the church, could have listened carefully to the sermon. Then he ended up running away from the law in Harvey Odum's maroon car.

She needed to have a long talk with him. To show him what it said in the Bible about stealing, if that was, in fact, what he'd done. "Who needs a little more dessert?"

"We got to get out of here," said the sheriff, standing. This could go on all day, he thought. Got to get untangled from all this.

"Well, I'm glad you-all could come by," said Mattie.

Robert looked at her. She's crazy, he thought. I'll have to call Elaine. Mama will have to get a checkup, some kind of mental checkup.

"It was mighty good," said Larry, standing. "Let's go," he said to Wesley.

"Where does he go next?" asked Laurie.

"To the station."

"I need to call my uncle," said Wesley.

"We've got to go now," said the sheriff.

"I'm allowed one phone call. The law allows me one phone call."

"Go ahead." I'm never going to get out of here, ever, he thought.

Wesley dialed Lamar's number. "Lamar, they got me. . . . Mrs. Rigsbee's. Yeah. . . . Yeah. . . . By the police station or somewhere, and then back to the RC, I guess."

XI

Everyone except Robert and Laurie had left.

Laurie was in the bathroom. She sat on the commode, looking at the space heater. What a strange meal, she thought. Robert certainly has an unusual family. Wesley seemed like he wanted to stay.

Robert sat at his place at the kitchen table. Mattie finished clearing the table.

"Do you want me to help you with that?" Robert asked.

"I'll get it. You sit still."

"Mother, I need to ask you something."

"Go ahead," said Mattie. She was gathering up the tablecloth.

"Have you been feeling all right?"

"Fine. Why?"

"I just wondered if . . ."

"What?"

"I just wondered . . ."

"I just feel bad about that boy having to go back to the RC and all. I feel sorry for him."

"Well, that boy don't feel sorry for you."

"How do you know?"

"Well, he . . . he, he's a thief, criminal, juvenile delinquent."

"I still feel sorry for him. Having to sit in that place and can't get out."

"That's the best place for him."

"He's never had a chance to hear the Gospel."

"What's that going to do for him?"

"Robert!" Mattie stopped and stared at her son.

"He's got as good a chance as anybody else to get the Gospel. They probably got Gideon Bibles all over the RC."

"Nobody ever loved him." Mattie held the tablecloth so no crumbs dropped out, and started for the back door.

"If they did he probably stole their car."

"Well. I don't know what to think." She stepped out into the backyard and shook out the tablecloth. Back inside, she said, "Matthew says—"

"Mother, I know what Matthew says."

"No, you don't. Not in a long time."

"Yes, I do. I listened to what Matthew said for twenty-three years."

"Well, you don't know what I'm fixing to say. I found it in Carrie's concordance while I was sitting in church today. 'Whatso ye do unto one of the least of these my brethren you do also to me.' And 'Whatso ye do not do to one of the least of these ye do not do unto me.' It was Jesus talking about people in prison. *In* prison. Wesley is certainly one of the least of these my brethren."

"I'll say." Robert sipped his coffee. "You've already done for him, Mama. You've already done I don't know what. Doesn't the Bible say when to stop?"

"No. Not that I know of. I've got to wash those dishes."

"I'll dry."

"I'll get it."

"No, let me help."

"I just . . . ," said Mattie.

"Anybody home?" said Pearl from the back door.

"Come on in," said Mattie.

As Pearl stepped up from the back step into the den, Laurie returned from the bathroom.

"How do you do?" said Laurie.

"What a pretty day out there," said Pearl. She saw Laurie. "Hello."

"This is Pearl Turnage, my sister," said Mattie. "And this is Laurie Thomas, Robert's friend."

"Nice to meet you. How are you all today?"

"Pretty good," said Robert. "I just survived the Alamo."

"Dominoes?"

"I just survived the *Alamo*."

"Oh. The Alamo."

"Come on over here, sit down, and eat a little pie and ice cream," said Mattie. "It has been something. I'll tell you all about it later."

"Oh, I don't need any pie and ice cream. But, my goodness, it does look good. Well, maybe just a little piece of
pie." She sat down at the table with Laurie and Robert.
"It's such a pretty day out there. Oh, before I forget it,"
she said to Mattie, "the stainless steels are in. Mr. Crosley
called."

"Good. But I'll be pretty busy next week getting ready
for the yard sale. Let's go the week after."

"Okay. Any time."

"Stainless steel what?" asked Robert.

"Caskets," said Mattie. "We went to look, but the
stainless steels won't in yet."

"Oh." I don't think I'll follow up on this one, thought
Robert, not with Laurie here.

"No need not to get that done while you can," said
Pearl. "Don't you think?" she asked Laurie.

"Oh, yes ma'am." What is she talking about? thought
Laurie.

"And what was your last name?" Pearl asked Laurie.

"Thomas."

"Ever know a Malley Thomas?"

"I've got a cousin named Malley."

"Won't Malley the one used to play fiddle?" said Mattie.

"He sure was," said Pearl. "Him and two others used
to play at square dances. Course that would be your
cousin's great-grandaddy or great-uncle or something,
I'll bet. Who were those other two fellows, Mattie?"

"Leed Stone and, ah, Press King," said Mattie, setting
ice cream and pie in front of Pearl. "Press was the one
had asthma so bad he couldn't sleep in a bed. Had to
sleep like he was in a barber chair."

"No," said Pearl, "I think that was Malley. Anyway, they used to play after the ball games they had down at the . . . at the, ah, what was the name of that field down below the Barn field?"

"Let's see," said Mattie. "I can't remember. What was it?"

"The fields had names?" asked Robert.

"You've heard me call the names of fields," said Mattie.

"I sure don't remember it."

"Oh yes," said Pearl. "All the fields around where we lived was named." She spooned pie and ice cream.

"What were some of the names?" asked Laurie.

"Well," Pearl swallowed. "Across the road was the Barn field and then heading down the hill was the one I was just trying to remember. Once you got to the bottom of the hill was the Corner field and then down the path to the mill was the Branch field."

"Old man Oakley used to burn the hillside of that Branch field every fall," Mattie said, "so in the spring, strawberries would grow as big as the end of your thumb. They came back every spring."

"What *was* the name of that field?" asked Pearl.

"Let's see . . . I can't remember."

"*All* the fields were named?" said Robert.

"Oh sure," said Pearl. "Every one."

"Just beyond the Branch field," said Mattie, "you turned off, and back in there was the House field, named after the old lady lived in there, Mildred House. The only way she could kill a chicken was catch it before it got off the roost, hold it between her legs and choke it to death."

"Didn't they used to chop their heads off?" asked Laurie.

"Chop it off or wring it," said Robert.

"Hers was a unusual method," said Pearl.

"What was the name of that field, Pearl?" asked Mattie.

"Well, let's see. I can't remember. It'll come to me. Anyhow, beyond the House field was the Hogarty field, wadn't it?"

"Yeah. And let's see. On the other side of the road was Buzzard field—close to the old buzzard rock, and up from that was the Medlin field."

"And across from that's the one we're trying to think of. It's where we were when Tom Sikes told you your legs were skinny," said Pearl.

"Yeah, and I went running in to Grandma and told her Tom Sikes said my legs were skinny, and she says, 'Well, honey, they are a mite thin.'"

"I've heard about that a few times," Robert said to Laurie. "But I didn't know about naming the fields."

"I wish I could remember the name of that one," said Pearl.

The front doorbell rang.

"I'll get it," said Robert.

"It'll come to us. One of us," said Mattie.

"This is very interesting," said Laurie. "You should have been here earlier, Mrs. Turnage. This has been a very interesting day."

Robert answered the door and came back in with Harvey Odum, who had come for his car.

"It just burns me up," Harvey was saying to Robert,

"stole out of the church parking lot. Hey, Miss Pearl, Miss Mattie."

"This is Laurie Thomas," said Robert. "Harvey Odum."

"Howdy, Miss Thomas. And I swear I hadn't left the key in the car over five times in my entire life."

Harvey, a short man, smoothed down his very sparse hair with his hand. He wore a bow tie. Harvey was always in charge of lighting the Christmas tree at church. "I'm sorry you had to get involved in all this, Miss Mattie," said Harvey.

"Don't worry about that, Harvey. I'm sorry this happened to you."

"I am too. But I'm glad they found the car. Except it does give you a funny feeling—like somebody's been through your dresser drawers or something like that; hard to explain if you ain't had something like this happen to you. I hope it ain't banged up in any way."

"It's out here," said Robert.

"That's a stolen car?" asked Pearl.

"Well, they think maybe so, yes. By the boy I visited last Sunday."

"Your little boyfriend from the prison?"

Boyfriend? thought Laurie. This gets *more* strange, she thought.

Harvey walked out into the backyard. They all followed him.

Harvey walked around the car, inspecting. "Looks okay on the outside."

"Looks like new," said Mattie.

"Wonder why he brought it over here? You say you visited him or something?"

"I know him," said Mattie.

Harvey stopped and looked at Mattie. "Is that right? You know him?"

"He had dinner over here," said Robert. "Just now."

"Dinner?"

"Well, the sheriff was here, too," said Mattie.

"One of the deputies had dinner, too," said Robert.

"Just about everybody had dinner," said Laurie.

"They were having dinner over here? With the boy that stole the car?!" asked Harvey.

"He was at church, too," said Robert.

"At church? Well, I know he was at church. That's where he stole my car from."

"No. He was in church," said Robert. "In the choir."

"I couldn't make out who it was," said Mattie.

"In the choir? Was that him? I do declare. I wondered. . . . I saw the two fellows come in, then leave."

"One of them, the young one, is the one took the car," said Mattie. "It gets kind of complicated."

"It does, don't it. I'm just glad to get my car back." Harvey bent and looked at the interior. "Looks like he didn't do it no damage inside, thank God. And there's the keys."

"I wouldn't have thought he would damage it," said Mattie. "I think he meant to borrow it and bring it back and leave it here for you to pick up."

"He *stole* it, Mama."

"So that was him in church," said Harvey. "I be doggone."

"That's right," said Robert.

"And he had dinner here? He just had dinner here?"

"That's right."

Harvey got into the car, put his hand on the key. "You some kin to him or something?" Harvey looked up at Mattie.

"He thinks I'm his grandma."

"His grandma?" Harvey kept his hand on the key but didn't turn it. "You're not, are you?"

Laurie, standing behind Mattie, shook her head back and forth.

"Oh no, but he needs one," said Mattie.

Pearl started inside for a dip of snuff.

Harvey cranked the car. "I tell you, this steering wheel feels dirty, somehow. Know what I mean?" he said to Robert. He put the gear shift in reverse and started backing away. "Well, I'll be seeing you all."

"Harvey!" called Mattie.

Harvey braked the LeBaron. Mattie approached his window. "The boy's in right much trouble. If you can find it in your heart not to press charges, I'd appreciate it. I'm trying to get him to turn around."

"Turn around? Well, Miss Mattie, I'd have to, ah, think real hard about that. He deserves the right punishment is the way I see it."

After everyone left, Mr. O'Brien, the preacher, called Mattie. He wanted to know how Mattie was holding up after the kidnapping; would she press charges, and what could he do? Mattie told him there wasn't a kidnapping, there wasn't a thing he could do, but if he wanted to come around one day during the week she'd fix him a little something to eat and talk about it. She might feel like talking to him about it. Or maybe he could come to the yard sale at Pearl's on Saturday. She had a pretty busy week in front of her with the canning she needed to do, along with getting ready for the yard sale.

Mr. O'Brien said he might do that, but if she needed him before then to be sure to call. Then he said a short prayer over the phone.

Mattie liked Mr. O'Brien all right, but not as much as the former preacher, Mr. Bass. Mr. Bass would come in your house, sit for a while, stand up, walk into the kitchen and go in your refrigerator without asking. And you wouldn't hold it against him one bit.

At 9:30 Mattie sat down at the piano and played "What a Friend We Have in Jesus," "This Is My Father's World," "There Is a Fountain," and "To a Wild Rose." She stood, sat back down, played and sang "Shall We Gather at the River," then "Victory in Jesus."

Sitting at her dresser, she squirted Jergens lotion onto her hands, rubbed them together. She noticed for the first time in a long time how her fingers were bent, the little ones mainly. She tried to straighten one. It looks like they would hurt, she thought, but they don't. She thought about Wesley. He was better off because of her. One reason Jesus wanted you to minister to those kind was that you couldn't lose. Next, she rubbed Pond's onto her hands and then onto her face while she looked into the mirror. She pictured Wesley back inside the RC. He might tell somebody that he stayed with his grandma over the weekend, that he ate Sunday dinner with her.

Why in the world were her own children so reluctant

to get married? What had she done wrong? Should she have taken them to movies showing people in love, happy marriages and all that? All this psychology. Well, there was no need to think about it. She'd done all right. They were good children. Never been in any trouble. They had jobs. She'd done all she could in keeping them clothed and fed and mothered, and she'd kept a husband clothed and fed, and sometimes mothered. She'd done a good job with all three.

She finished rubbing the Pond's onto her face. Tomorrow she'd have to start a week of collecting things from around the house for Saturday's yard sale. Or at least making some decisions about what she was going to have to take, take in Lamar's truck. She needed to call him. It was late, she'd call him tomorrow.

As Mattie was drifting off to sleep, the phone rang. It was Elaine.

"What in the world happened, Mother? Alora called and said there'd been a raid and I don't know what all— with this criminal in the house."

"There won't no raid. It was just a mess, a sort of a mess, with the nephew of the dogcatcher. Didn't you meet him? Saturday?"

"Oh, yes. I met him. Do you need me to come by?"

"No, everything's fine."

"Alora said they might charge you with aiding and abetting a criminal. She said he was an escaped convict."

"No, he's just from down the road at the RC. You knew that."

"Well, I'll come by Tuesday. Does Robert know?"

"He was here. Brought a young woman with him, but

we didn't get much of a chance to talk. I wish you could have met her. She was real nice."

"Maybe I'll get a chance. Look, I'll come by Tuesday. I want to hear all about what happened."

"Okay. You come on. You can help me decide what of yours to take to the yard sale Saturday."

"Okay, bye."

"Bye."

The phone rang again. It was Carrie. "Did he do anything to you, Mattie?"

"Oh, nobody did anything."

"Did he *try* to do anything—you know, anything funny?"

"Oh no, he's a right nice boy."

"Somebody said they had him in jail for rape."

"Oh no. No. No. I think all he did was take a car without asking. That's all. He's never had anybody much to look out after him. He's a right nice boy in some ways. Looks right nice, if he could get a little work done on his teeth."

"Then you're okay?"

"Oh yeah, I'm fine, Carrie. Thank you for calling." After hanging up, Mattie wondered about taking her phone off the hook but decided against it. She'd heard of people doing that. She knew Elaine did it sometimes. But you ought to keep the line open. Anybody should. Somebody sick might call. If you didn't want people calling, you ought not to get a phone. Nothing worse than to call Elaine, and get a busy signal, and you know her receiver is laying on the table, off the hook.

XII

Mr. O'Brien, the preacher, received a phone call from Clarence Vernon, the head deacon, at 10:15. After Clarence apologized for calling so late, they discussed what to do about Mattie Rigsbee's involvement with the young criminal.

"Well, the thing that bothers me," said Clarence, "is we got the convention coming up and Miss Mattie being a Sunday school officer and heading up the Lottie Moon, if this thing got out and she gets charged with something . . . Then, too, it could affect our membership drive. It's just a bunch of things all together. Not that I have anything against Miss Mattie—she's as fine a person as can be. You know what I mean."

They agreed to pray about it. Clarence then called

Beatrice. They decided that perhaps Beatrice should have a little talk with Mattie, that they were feeling the Lord's guidance.

To his fellow inmates Wesley described the girl who, driving an '84 Camaro, picked him up within two hours of his escape on Friday. She had money. Big money. Friday night they ate flaming food at the Radisson in High Point. Best food he'd ever had. They spent the night there. Best loving he'd ever had. The things she could do. Saturday she wanted to fly to Las Vegas, but he told her he had to meet Blake behind the 7-Eleven in Listre. They waited behind the 7-Eleven and Blake never showed. So they drove back to High Point and spent *Saturday* night at the Radisson. It was damned hard to believe that he could be so lucky. And she had money. Insisted on buying everything.

Sunday morning she wanted to go to church of all things—to church!—so he went along but the law was on his trail by this time, the FBI, and he fooled the hell out of them by putting on a choir deal and getting in the choir and then stealing a Cadillac, but they caught him in a chase which wrecked two highway patrol cars and he knew they wouldn't put that in the newspaper because he outmaneuvered the hell out of them, even in that big old Cadillac, which talked out of the dash and told you if your seat belt won't fastened.

Wesley told his story in the RC dining room over a supper of beans and franks, powdered potatoes, canned string beans, white bread, and canned peaches for dessert.

After lights out, Wesley lay on his back in his upper bunk with his hands behind his head. He stared through a barred window on the opposite wall at an outside flood-light, normally activated by darkness, now malfunctioning, blinking off and on. He thought about Patricia, how she wouldn't let him do anything hardly, even after he told her he loved her and that she was the most beautiful girl he'd ever known.

He thought about his grandma. He was, after all, from good blood, tough blood. She could cook better than anybody he'd ever known. He'd never known a piece of pound cake could be so moist and solid and sweet. Those biscuits were light and tasty and that cornbread crisp and hard on the outside, mushy on the inside. She was a magician.

The light outside blinked out completely. Somebody farted. The light came back on.

Maybe she would agree to keep him. That lawyer had said that if he could get a respectable relative to sign for him, then . . . He'd ask her on Sunday, if she came to visit, if him and Blake hadn't already got out by then.

After Carrie's call Mattie couldn't go to sleep. She kept seeing the weekend as some kind of odd movie in her head. There was the church, the warm, waiting church with Wesley in it. She had counted on it changing him somehow. It was such a warm, welcoming place, so home-like; but Wesley had just sort of flitted through with the deputies after him, got stuck in the choir. It hadn't had time to do anything to him. It hadn't taken. But she shouldn't expect so much in so little time. He needed to go several times. If she could just get him out of the RC on Sundays and into the church, and do that for about three months, then maybe it would take.

She pulled the short chain on the headboard lamp, sat on the side of the bed, reached for her housecoat, then sweater, put them on, pushed her feet into her slippers, stood and walked to the kitchen, turning on the bedroom light so she could see in the hall, the hall light so she could see in the kitchen. In the almost-dark kitchen, she got a biscuit from the bread pan, broke it in half, put one half back, and put the lid on the pan. She opened the refrigerator to its bright light and hum, got out the quart carton of milk and poured half a glass. She remembered when they changed the spout on the milk cartons. The spout had been simple; you pulled open a little hole and poured your milk. Then they'd changed it so you had to to do all that work. The first time she used the new spout she had the hardest time getting it open; then when she did, she used the same angle—for distance—she would have used with the old-style spout and the milk poured right over the top of the glass onto the table. She thought of that so often. Robert remembered and mentioned it sometimes. When it happened—so long ago—he'd laughed and laughed.

Mattie remembered how she fixed raw eggs and chocolate milk for Robert, Elaine, and Paul. One raw egg a day for each of them, beat up in a glass of chocolate milk. Paul had complained as much as the children—but it put some color in their cheeks and made them feel better whether they believed it or not.

She ate the half biscuit and drank the milk. She remembered how Paul would get up, walk to the kitchen, eat a piece of cheese and a piece of pound cake, drink a half glass of milk—only a *half* glass to keep him from having to get up later in the night to go to the bathroom; but he'd have to get up anyway. He might as well have had a full glass. And he always woke her up when he got up. She'd get mad about that but never told him of course, and then she'd started having to get up once a night herself. Sometimes lately she didn't miss him from the couch or from the kitchen table. But in the bed, his absence was always there.

She took the last bite of biscuit, the last swallow of milk, stood, swept the crumbs into her hand, put them into the bird bowl, rinsed the glass, set it in the sink, and went to bed.

On Monday morning at ten, Sheriff Tillman came by—holding a clipboard and a pad—to see Mattie. He needed to ask a few questions. While he asked questions, he and Mattie sat at the kitchen table with cups of coffee. He wrote down what Mattie said.

Mattie said she got to know Wesley through the dogcatcher who cut her out of her rocking chair, she didn't know anything about how he escaped, she did visit him because she realized he was somebody she could help, one of the least of these my brethren, and the reason she hadn't pointed Wesley out was because the choir was too far away for her to see who was up there.

"The choir?"

"Oh me."

"He was in the choir when we were at the church?"

"Well, I don't rightly know. That's the rumor. But it don't seem to make much difference now."

"I'll check that out. One other thing," said the sheriff, writing. "Why do you think he came back here after he stole the car?"

"Pound cake, I imagine. He knew that's what I usually have and he likes it. Oh yes, it might have had something to do with the fact that he thinks I'm his grandma."

Sheriff Tillman looked up. "You're not, are you?"

Mattie looked at the sheriff over the rim of her coffee cup. "Oh no. I don't suppose so."

"Where'd he get that idea?"

"'Cause I went to visit him; and I'm certainly old enough. He just put all that together. I think he has a lively imagination."

"Did you tell him you won't his grandma?"

"Not exactly."

"Did you tell him you was."

"Sort of, I guess."

"You probably ought to tell him you ain't, next time you see him."

"I guess so."

"He told me you was." The sheriff stood with the clipboard in his hand, stuck his pen in his shirt pocket. "Well, I think that'll do it, Mrs. Rigsbee. You obviously aren't involved in this in any direct way. I didn't think you would be, but this is my job; got to have it all down on paper, you know."

"I know. You're supposed to ask questions. I'm glad I got to meet you. I see your picture in the paper every once in a while. Do you have any children?"

"Oh, yeah, three. They keep me busy." He stepped out on the back step. "You take it easy now."

"Okay. Come back when you can stay awhile."

In the kitchen, Mattie poured cookie crumbs from the cookie jar into the bird bowl with the biscuit crumbs from the night before. Three children. She crumbled up the biscuit half she hadn't eaten, put that in, and walked to the back door. There came Alora across the backyard, looking worried. Mattie stood on the step and scattered the crumbs, spoke to Alora. Alora followed her into the house.

"What did the sheriff want?" asked Alora.

"He just had a few questions. How long I'd known Wesley and so forth, if I knew how he escaped."

"Did you know?"

"No, I didn't. Wesley told me he was on leave."

"I declare it's upset me terrible. I've started sleeping with my gun now."

"Sleeping with it? Under the pillow?"

"Yes. Don't tell that boy, if you go back out there to see him."

"No, no, I wouldn't tell him that, but I don't think he would harm a flea."

"He's a thief. There's nothing worse than a thief. You just don't know *what* a thief will do. I probably shouldn't have told you about sleeping with the gun."

"I won't tell him. You want a cup of coffee?"

"It could slip out though. And he might want a gun and break in and try to steal it. No, I don't want any coffee. I got to get on back. Don't tell Finner either."

"Tell him what?"

"That I got a gun under my pillow."

"He don't know?"

"He thinks one is enough, but I don't feel safe with one under just his pillow. Mr. Lowry gave a talk Wednesday night at prayer meeting about secular humanists. He said they were all over the place."

"What are they, anyway? I keep reading about them."

"Well, they do all these secular things for one thing and you just don't know when one's liable to break in your bedroom and start doing some of it."

"I just read something about one the other day somewhere," said Mattie. "I'm not going to worry about them. You sure you don't want a cup of coffee?" Mattie needed to start getting things ready for the yard sale on Saturday. She wished Alora would go on back. A little bit each day, putting stuff in piles, and she'd be all ready by Saturday.

"No, I got to get on back and do some cleaning."

"I got to get stuff ready for the yard sale Saturday. Pearl is going to have it, and me and whoever else. I'm going to try to clear out all the stuff I don't need. You got anything you want to sell, you can join us."

"Where's it going to be?"

"In Pearl's yard—more traffic by there."

"Let's see, I got a floor lamp I want to get rid of—that Mexican rifle with a lightbulb in the end of the barrel, and a great big shade. I'm so tired of it I don't know what to do. Finner has had it for forty years. Bought it in Mexico. The thing is, with all those little bolts and stuff it collects dust and I'm tired of dusting it. You dust a rifle lamp for forty years, you get tired of it."

I'll have to worry over it and bring her back the money, thought Mattie. "Why don't you get up a bunch of things and go with us? I'm going to call Lamar, the dogcatcher, to pick up my stuff in his pickup; he could swing by and get you and your stuff, too."

"I don't know. I'll think about it. I'll bring the lamp over anyway. You might be able to sell it."

"Don't you want a bite to eat?" I declare, she's going to sit right here through my dinner, thought Mattie.

"Oh, no, I got to get on back. I got a lot to do this morning. I'm sorry about the sheriff having to come and all that," said Alora, leaving. "I'll give you a call if I decide to do the yard sale."

"Okay, just let me know." Mattie walked over and looked in the refrigerator. Maybe she'd just fix a sandwich. She had that pimiento cheese. She could eat by 12:30 and have thirty minutes to do a little survey, decide what she wanted to take to the yard sale. She could do that before her program came on.

She warmed string beans and made a cucumber sandwich instead of pimiento cheese.

At 12:30 she went into Robert's room. Those encyclopedias could go. Somebody might want them. But they were so old. Late forties, and Elaine carried the W to school and lost it. But coming right before XYZ, maybe nobody would notice. If they did, she'd give them a dollar off.

The desk. The little desk she and Paul gave Robert for his seventh birthday. She knew what was in each drawer: bottom left, arrowheads; middle left, Instamatic camera which didn't work, one of two he owned—she'd been after him for a least twenty years to fix one of them. Top left, pictures of Robert and Bobby Larkin and all the Larkin dogs; top middle, binoculars, marionette head, a ruler, pencils; top right, three baseballs and a leather wallet with a tractor-trailer truck carved into it, made by a prisoner; middle right, his Boy Scout hunting knife, three compasses and the other broken Instamatic camera; bottom right, a baseball signed by all the Durham Bulls, two Indian headbands, and a sailor cap.

She wouldn't take the desk. It would be so nice for a grandson or granddaughter who would be happy to have all those things in the drawers to look at, to get Robert to remember and tell about. She wished she had things from her childhood to talk about, but of course she hadn't had anything much, and went to work when she was thirteen. She'd never had toys except what her daddy made. And several dolls, except once after a revival her mother had made her and Pearl throw away all their dolls and books.

She would take one of those Instamatic cameras and sell it for a dollar.

And there were those other books. Those Spanish books she'd bought Robert after he made a D. A grandson or granddaughter could certainly use those. They were nice little books, but Robert had never used them. And in the cigar box: medals and certificates of achievement. If Robert had a son or daughter they'd appreciate all of that. If she gave the cigar box to Robert he'd lose it or throw it away and then if he ever had a child he'd wish he'd kept it. He could easily have a child—as long as he married somebody younger than himself.

But he'd better hurry; she'd just read somewhere that sperm from a man over forty-four started losing its freshness. She'd been reading so much about sperm lately. Used to be you didn't read the first thing about sperm, but it had got so you read about it in *Reader's Digest* even. It used to be you could count on them to keep out that kind of thing.

She'd better go see what time it was. It was almost time for her program.

While Mattie was cleaning her dishes after "All My Children," she heard a truck drive up. It was Lamar. Good. They could talk about what all happened yesterday. She watched him take a windowpane out to Finner and Alora's garage and put it in, walk back to the truck and get some papers from his front seat. He came in, said he had only a minute, that he was just passing by and had all these legal guardian papers that some caseworker had sent him a few months ago and that there was no way he could take on Wesley, he didn't have room, but he was just wondering . . . the thought struck him that maybe Mattie could take on Wesley—legal guardian. She had right much room; all she'd have to do is sign the papers and if that Mr. Odum didn't press charges, they'd probably let him out early. Wesley could get a job, rent a room from her, and it would be a little extra income for her. "You want to look the papers over?"

"Lord have mercy. I can't keep somebody here. No sir. It does get lonesome, you know, but you get used to living by yourself. And I'm slowing down. I couldn't keep somebody here."

"I don't blame you, but this caseworker keeps sending

stuff, and I didn't know. You can just keep it and look at it."

"Well, I ain't even able to keep a dog with all there is to do around here. Let me ask you something before you go. We're going to have a yard sale Saturday, me and Pearl and one or two more, and if you're going to be running around in your truck—it's going to be over at Pearl's, and do you reckon you might pick up a few things from here? I probably won't be able to get it all in my car. I'm aiming to get rid of a lot of stuff and if there are some things you want—I'm getting rid of some of Paul's things—you can have them."

"Paul?"

"My husband. He died four, no five years ago. Four? No, I guess it was five, and I still got some of his things."

"Yeah, I'll do it." Lamar thought of shoes, wing tips; he needed wing tips. "What size shoes did he wear?"

"Shoes? Ten, I think. Let's go see."

Later that afternoon, Mattie was cutting the grass in her backyard on the bank which descended down to a woods path. The bank was steep. She used to do the whole yard in one day, but had given up on that. She was thinking about how if Wesley lived with her, he could do the grass and she wouldn't have to worry about it; but he wouldn't trim, for sure. You couldn't get anybody who would trim. She'd tried several boys, but they all did an awful job. It took her half a day to go around behind them trimming. She might as well do it all herself. She enjoyed the exercise. She *ought* to do her own grass.

As she made her turn at the bottom of the bank she

saw Beatrice standing near the back door, watching. She stopped, cut off the lawnmower, and started up the bank. "Well, how you doing, Beatrice?" she called.

"Fine. I didn't want to scare you. Just thought I'd stop by for a little visit. I was in the neighborhood."

"Let's go over here and sit." About four more strips and I'd been through, thought Mattie. What in the world? Beatrice has never visited me in her life.

They walked to the metal lawn chairs.

Mattie went on inside, and poured two glasses of iced tea, tore off a paper towel for Beatrice, picked up a used one for herself, came back outside, handed Beatrice her tea, and sat down.

"That's a lot of work, cutting the grass," said Beatrice.

"Well, it is, but I give myself two days to do it now. I used to do it in one." I bet she's never cut a blade of grass in her life, thought Mattie. Beatrice had attended college in Virginia and saw to it that everybody knew, over and over.

"What I came for is to say I'm sorry about all that in Sunday school. I couldn't imagine you knew that boy was escaped."

"Well, no, I didn't. I . . . it was just all a big mix-up."

"And another thing—I wanted to ask you about our new member from Maryland. To ask you if you'd do something for us."

"What's that?"

"Well, she was the president of her Sunday school class where she's from and what I was wondering is, since the vice-president doesn't do all that much anyway, what I was wondering is if maybe we could let her have that office so she would, you know, feel included. She's been coming for about a month and hasn't joined yet, and we can use everybody we can get in the membership drive and I just believe that if she had an office in the Sunday school department then she'd join the church, transfer her membership, and we'd have a new member for the membership drive and then too she wouldn't have to feel left out, you know, in our department. Just think about it. It was just a little something I thought about that we might could do."

"Oh . . . well, it's okay with me, I guess, but since it's an office, we'd have to have somebody nominate her and vote her in and all. What's her name—Elizabeth?"

"Elizabeth Fisher. I think we could work that out."

"I see what you mean. Help her feel at home and all. Well, I suppose it's okay with me."

"Okay," said Beatrice, "I'll see what the others say and bring it up on Sunday if that's all right with you."

"It's fine with me. I'll be working on the Lottie Moon, anyway. Let me get you some more tea."

"I don't think I want any more, thank you. I don't have but a minute. And like I say, I am sorry about all your trouble Sunday."

"Well, it was a kind of funny thing. That boy is right pitiful in a way. He's never had much of a chance at anything. Lived at Berry Hill Orphanage all his life, got in trouble and ended up at the YMRC. I didn't have no idea at all when he come by here on Saturday that he'd escaped."

"It's just awful, what goes on nowadays," said Beatrice. "Everybody's getting divorced and you never know what's going to happen, or where it's going to happen, or who it's going to happen to, do you?"

"No. No, you don't."

"I wonder about how strong the church is in the middle of it all. It seems like the state has just about taken over everything." Beatrice stood. "I pray about it, but I declare, sometimes I don't even know what to pray."

"I know. Me either." He would have to learn to put things back where he got them, thought Mattie. I wouldn't go around picking up after him like I did with Robert and Elaine.

"Well, it was good to see you, Mattie," said Beatrice as she left. "Just think about this little vice-presidency thing. We'll talk about it Sunday."

"Okay." I could *teach* him how to trim. The importance of trimming so that it looks good—not so shaggy around the trees and up against the house.

XIII

Elaine came by to see Mattie late Tuesday afternooon.
No, Mattie said, she wasn't feeling funny. She felt good.
Yes, everything was fine about Sunday. It had just been a
misunderstanding. Would she please go in her room and
put out everything she wanted sold at the yard sale
Saturday.

Elaine spent two hours sifting, looking at old scrap-
books and pictures, reading a diary, then letters from an
old boyfriend.

Thursday night Mattie called Lamar to be sure he remembered about Saturday morning. He said he would
be there with the truck by 7:30. If he ate breakfast with
her, that would put them in Pearl's yard at eight, eight-

fifteen or so. Alora had decided to come at nine, bring
Finner's Mexican rifle lamp and a few other things.

On Friday night Clarence Vernon, the head deacon,
ate the chicken and dumplings, string beans, and potatoes his wife had fixed. He ate quietly. His wife wouldn't
understand if he tried to explain what he had to do on
Sunday. He was going to have to straighten out the Mattie Rigsbee business. For the sake of the church. He
knew exactly how to handle it. He would tell Mattie how
much he appreciated what she had done for the church
and also for this unfortunate young man. The thief. De-
generate, evil boy. But he would have to point out that it
seemed to him as head deacon that the line had been
crossed. You cannot take in, support, protect, hide, con-
spire with a known criminal. You can treat him well in
prison, the Scriptures even speak of that, but anything
beyond that is wrong; beyond that is where the Devil
comes in. It's clear. He would say he thought it would be
best for her to give up the Lottie Moon until the whole
business blew over—until all charges of wrongdoing
had settled down appropriately.

He liked Mattie Rigsbee, and would be sure to tell her
so, and he'd be sure to ask her opinion about the whole
thing. But his calling was not to Mattie Rigsbee, it was
to higher offices: Duty, the Church, God.

By the time Clarence went to bed, Mattie had five
piles throughout her house, ready to go to the yard sale
the next morning: a Robert pile, an Elaine pile, a Paul
pile, a Mattie pile, and a miscellaneous pile. She had
called Elaine and Robert and given them one last chance

at their goods. Robert wanted Mattie to keep his arrow-heads, that was it. Elaine said she had brought all she wanted to her apartment. She was going to Chapel Hill for a conference and would stop by the yard sale. A man named Winston Sullivan would be with her.

When Mattie sat down to the piano Friday night, she had a vague sense that some sort of trade-off was coming. Maybe it was that she was getting rid of some of Elaine's old things, her childhood things, roller skates, her last two dolls, a watercolor set, and in exchange Elaine was bringing a young man to the yard sale for her to meet. Well, he might be young. He could be old, with Elaine there at thirty-eight already. Elaine hadn't brought any-body to meet in about a year. This was a good sign. And so soon after Robert had brought somebody.

And she was getting rid of some of Robert's old things. She could call Robert and see if he'd bring that nice young lady to the yard sale to meet this Winston Sullivan fellow. She'd like for the four of them to get together, to spend some time together. Maybe she could have them all to Sunday dinner. If not this Sunday then the next. She'd ask Elaine tomorrow. But tomorrow they could all have a good time talking about the toys for sale, remembering.

Mattie thumbed through the hymnbook. She found and played "Blest Be the Tie," and then "Morning Has Broken." She played "To a Wild Rose" once. She hummed "Walking Across Egypt," but still couldn't remember the words. It was in one of those old songbooks she'd gotten out of the piano bench to sell. Too late to go through all that. She'd get Robert and Elaine and Laurie and that Winston Sullivan to go on a little treasure hunt for it.

That would be fun. Something for them to do together— see who could find "Walking Across Egypt" first. Then she'd bring it home and they could all sing it together around the piano sometime.

She went to the kitchen and got the papers on Wesley and sat down with them on the couch in the den. She read, noticing the blank spaces where you had to fill in your name, address, schooling, dates. Schooling? Well, if she decided to keep him, she could put something in. It had been so long ago. You agreed to provide for the physical needs, to provide guidance, to know where he was at all times. Stapled to the form was a paper of some sort which said chances for guardianship would be increased if the guardian was a relative.

It would be a nice challenge for her to get that boy started on another road, another path, in another direction. Get his teeth fixed, buy him some clothes, get him going to church, back in school.

But she wouldn't be able to do as much as she could when she was younger. She didn't have the energy; she was slowing down.

Well . . . she needed to go ahead and pray about it and make a decision: either yes, so she could get on with it, or no, so she could put it out of her head for good.

He could have Robert's room. She wouldn't have to buy a thing. She had several sets of sheets. She could get one of those Instamatics fixed for him, too.

Sitting on the couch with the legal papers in her lap, the lamp lighted beside her, she closed her eyes and prayed. Dear Lord, bless this house and all I try to do.

Guide and protect me in making this decision. Help me to do what is right.

What if *everybody* did good unto the least of these? thought Mattie. What in the world would happen? But that would only happen if the Devil went away somehow. It's up to Christians to lead the way, to do what's right. But I'm not young anymore, able to take on this, that, and the other. It's getting harder just to keep up this house. I need to look after myself—do a good job of that. I owe that to myself. I can't take care of some boy who's liable to do no telling what.

Dear gentle Jesus, guide me in making this decision. I need to get it over with, decide now. Please guide and direct me. In Thy precious name. Amen.

Mattie looked across the den into the kitchen, dark except for the light from the lamp beside her. What if Wesley was sitting over there right now doing something he ought not to be doing: eating hard candy, or worse still, drinking a beer. What would she say? She'd talk to him and explain. Maybe take more time to explain than she used to take with Robert and Elaine.

She closed her eyes. Now was the time. How could she do it? Well, it had to be some sort of instant decision, something quick. There was just no way she could *figure* it out. It would have to come in a flash.

She had an idea. She pictured herself standing in the pulpit looking out into the church sanctuary. The church was empty except for three little . . . little ghostlike figures, sitting in the middle of the auditorium on her right, and three in the middle on her left. Mattie spoke to the three on her right. "If I am to keep Wesley, you three stand up—when the time comes," she said. She looked at the three on her left. "If I am *not* to keep Wesley, you three stand up when the time comes. All of you take your time. Don't move until you have to. Now. Do what you have to do." She stood before them, watching and waiting.

Together, the three on the right stood. Mattie opened her eyes.

That was that.

She looked at the papers in her hands. She let her head fall back. She looked at the water stain on the ceiling. She needed to shout out. A big upside-down waterfall seemed to be flowing up out of her—up out of her head. "Amen," she said loudly. She was going to have a boarder. What in the world would Pearl say? "Amen," she said again. She stood, raised her hands. "Amen." And then: "*Hester* field." She remembered! She'd have to call Pearl, tell her she remembered the name of the field, and see what she thought about her big decision. Pearl would go along. She might resist a little to start with, but she'd go along eventually. Alora. Lord, Alora might shoot him. Alora or Finner, one.

She felt a great rush of energy. She felt wonderful. She needed to call somebody and tell them. Pearl? No, it was too late.

"Hello, Elaine?"

"Hi, Mother. I've got company; can I call you back tomorrow?"

"Company? This late?"

"Mother, it's just, ah, 10:15."

"A man?"

"Yes, Mother. It's okay. I'm thirty-eight."

"How old is he?"

"I don't know. I hadn't thought about it."

"Ask him."

"Mother! What is this—the Spanish Inquisition?"

"I'm getting married."

"Say that again, Mother."

"I'm getting married."

"Mother, this is no time for jokes. I've got company."

"I'm getting married so I can have my own grand-children. I'm signing the papers tonight."

"Mother, that is ridiculous. What papers?!"

"The guardian papers."

"What are you talking about, Mother? What guardian papers?"

"The guardian papers on Wesley Benfield. So he can live here."

"*Wesley*. The juvenile delinquent? Mother, sit down. Are you sitting down?"

"I'm standing at the kitchen counter. I'm fine. I'm going to take him in and I'm prepared to say yes when he asks me to marry him. And I imagine he will."

"Mother, now stop it. If you don't stop it, I'm coming over there."

"Come on, and spend the night."

"I . . . Mother . . ."

"What's your friend's name? Is it the one you're planning to bring to the yard sale?"

"Winston Sullivan. Yes. He's the one."

"Let me speak to him."

"Mother! What for?"

"Let me speak to him."

"Just a minute."

"Hello."

"Mr. Sullivan?"

"Yes."

"Do you have any intention of marrying Elaine?"

"Well, I, ah, haven't gotten quite that far in my thinking, ah, about things."

"Well, if you don't marry her I'm going to marry a sixteen-year-old boy and have my own grandchildren, even if I have to rent them, or adopt them, or whatever it is."

"Oh. Well, I'm not sure I understand."

"You understand what marriage is, don't you?"

"Oh yes, but—"

"How's your sperm?"

"Beg your pardon?"

"I said how's your sperm; how old are you?"

"I'm forty-seven. I hadn't checked my sper—"

"Your sperm starts getting weak when you pass forty-four."

"Mrs. Rigsbee, I don't feel comfortable talking to you about this. I—"

"Let me speak to Elaine."

"Yes. Okay. Good night, Mrs. Rigsbee."

"Good night. Sleep tight."

Winston looked at the phone and handed it to Elaine.

"Hello, mother?"

"He sounds like a nice young man but it's time he was

going home. Or getting married. His sperm is getting tired."

"Mother, what in the world has happened to you? Do you feel all right?"

"I feel wonderful. I feel like a upside-down waterfall is coming up out of my head."

"Oh? Well, listen. You go to bed right now. And we'll see you tomorrow. Get some rest. Right now. You're not going to marry anybody, for goodness sakes, Mother. Let's talk about all this tomorrow."

"Fine. We'll all talk tomorrow. And find 'Walking Across Egypt' and bring it home and all sing it together."

"Okay. Bye, Mother."

"Bye-bye."

Elaine hung up the phone and stood looking at Winston Sullivan. "She's lost her mind. I've got to do something. I'll have to call Robert."

Mattie turned out the kitchen light, walked into the hall and on down toward her bedroom. She turned on the bedroom light, turned out the hall light. What in the world? What a funny conversation. *Somebody* needed to get married.

XIV

The morning sun glowed orange through the top of a black pine tree as Lamar turned into Mattie's driveway. She would have hot coffee and no telling what to eat. Some of those biscuits. And maybe he could get another pair of shoes. Those wing tips fit perfect.

He stepped onto the back steps and knocked on the door. No one answered. He started around to the front.

The back door opened. Mattie stuck her head out. "Come on in. I was in the bathroom. I been so excited I got up at five."

Lamar stepped into the den.

"Take off your hat," said Mattie. "I've got something to tell you." She picked up the papers off the counter. "See these papers, the guardian papers; well, I signed them last night and I feel just as good about it this morning as I did then. Take off your hat."

"Well, slap my thigh."

Mattie walked to the stove. "You want some breakfast, don't you?"

"Sure."

"How do you want your eggs?"

"Scrambled. I'll be doggone."

"Yep. I decided to get on with it. Have a seat there at the table."

"Wesley'll be happy. He'll be real happy. I hope they let him out."

"Well, I do too. We'll call him up in a little bit." Mattie placed butter on the table. "How about that little dog? Is he still at the pound?"

"Yeah. I've seen him a few times."

"Well, I'm trying to decide—maybe I ought to get him back. Wesley'll need something around to look after, to take care of. That'll do him good, don't you think?"

"Oh, yeah. I can bring him to you anytime."

"Well, I don't know. Let me see how things go with Wesley, then we'll worry about the dog. One thing at a time. Maybe I ought to get a parakeet. Take off your hat."

Lamar took off his hat. Mattie handed him his plate, sat at the table herself, took a sip of coffee.

Lamar buttered his biscuit. "Ain't you going to say the blessing?" he asked.

"Oh yes. Thank you, Lord for these and the many blessings Thou hast given us. In Thy precious name, amen."

Lamar took a bite of egg, biscuit. "You never named that dog, did you?" he asked.

"Oh no."

"He ain't got but about two weeks before they do him in."

"We'll know something before then."

216 Walking Across Egypt

WORDS AND MUSIC: CLYDE EDGERTON

ARR.: BARBARA PENICK

1. Walk - ing across E - gypt, no shel - ter from the sun. My
2. Walk - ing across E - gypt, the dis - tance may be great. His
3. Walk - ing across E - gypt, to touch the face of God. The
4. Like Mo - ses we are walk-ing in - to the prom - ised land. We're

jour - ney has no stop - ping place. My jour - ney's far from done.
love will keep me walk - ing, bring - ing vic - tory o - ver hate.
least who are a - mong us place their feet where Je - sus trod.
walk - ing across E - gypt our hearts to - geth - er band. The

Walk - ing with Je - sus, I shall not stop to rest. My
Walk - ing with Je - sus, our chil - dren lead the way. Come
Je - sus' hand will lead us; and we shall ne - ver fear. His
bright hope of Je - sus has led us all the way.

faith is set be - fore me, and my jour - ney shall be blest.
join me in my jour - ney to the bright - est day.
love is here a - mong us and the jour - ney shall be dear.
Hand in hand we'll tra - vel to the bright - est day.

CHORUS

I'm walk-ing (walk-ing), walk-ing (walk-ing), walk-ing across E - gypt (walk-ing).

Walk-ing across E - gypt, My heart shall see the way. (My stride) My

stride shall not be bro - ken, there will be no de - lay.

Walk-ing with Je - sus to the bright - est day.

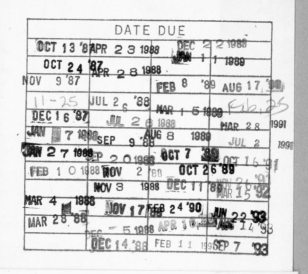